BOY GIRL BOY

BOY GIRL BOY

Ron Koertge

Harcourt, Inc.

Orlando   Austin   New York   San Diego   Toronto   London

www.HarcourtBooks.com

Headings with chapter openers by Gaylord Brewer from
Barbaric Mercies, copyright © 2003. Reprinted by permission of Red Hen Press,
Granada Hills, California.

Library of Congress Cataloging-in-Publication Data
Koertge, Ronald.
Boy girl boy/Ron Koertge.
p. cm.
Summary: Three troubled high school seniors, who plan to run away
together from Illinois to California after graduation, try to figure out
who they are and who they want to be.
[1. Friendship—Fiction. 2. Self-perception—Fiction.
3. Homosexuality—Fiction.] I. Title.
PZ7.K8187Bg 2005
[Fic]—dc22 2004030021
ISBN-13: 978-0152-05325-3 ISBN-10: 0-15-205325-5

Text set in Bembo
Designed by Cathy Riggs

First edition
A C E G H F D B
Printed in the United States of America

For Bianca and Jan

Consider thyself to be dead, and to have completed thy life up to the present time; and live according to nature the remainder which is allowed thee.

—MARCUS AURELIUS

BOY GIRL BOY

1

*Everything looks different
told from different ways.*

ELLIOT

I am hot! Nothing but net from everywhere. Okay, it's my driveway and nobody's got his hand in my face, but this is amazing. Fifteen in a row, the last one from the middle of the street. I wish that jerk who wrote *Slow release, slow feet* on a scouting report could see me now.

When I was little, I slept with my basketball. Mom's got a picture of me in my Spidey pajamas, both arms around my first Rawlings. Maybe I'm not the fastest guy in the world, but nobody takes the ball away from me.

I wish I didn't have to meet Mary Ann. Or maybe I just wish I didn't have to meet her in the pasture. I for sure can't go until I miss. No way am I stopping when I'm on a run like this.

Well...

Nobody could have made that last one. Now I can

trudge down there. Up Huron Street, cut past Mr. Denby's house; go by the falling-down-on-itself shed where Mr. Tieman kept plow horses about a thousand years ago, cross the barbed wire fence, then pick up the path that zigzags down toward the little stream Teresa used to pretend was the Nile.

Oh, man. The view from here used to be so cool: up to my ankles in fescue, big stand of maple trees, and a few cows with those black-and-white sides like seat covers.

And now? More little stakes with more orange ribbons. I come down here at night, pull them up, and throw them away. Next morning they're back. What do they do—multiply in the dark? Now they're almost to the Volvo. Our Volvo.

I dial Larry on my new cell. I point like he was right beside me. "Can you believe this?"

"It's not even ten a.m., Elliot. I'm vulnerable. I can believe anything."

"I'm down in the pasture. Waiting for Mary Ann. What do you think would happen if I laid down in front of the bulldozers?"

"That's *lay* down, Elliot, and anyway they'd run over you. Did you finish your *Gatsby* essay?"

"Teresa's proofing it. Listen, Mary Ann's on her way, but where are you going to be in twenty minutes?"

"Twenty minutes? The girls on *The View* are right: Romance is dead."

"She said she just wants to talk."

"I'll be here for a little while. I'm watching this movie on HBO."

"I'm gonna call Teresa. I'll tell her to meet me at your house, okay? We'll do something."

"Don't we always?"

I hit the little End button to finish the call. Larry's always watching a movie. Or part of one, anyway. He's funny that way. We've been friends forever, though. Me, him, and Teresa. They're the only ones I've got in my phone book.

I punch #2 and don't even give her a chance to say anything. "Hey, have you seen the pasture?"

"Hello to you, too."

"Well, have you seen it?"

"Sure, Larry and I tried to figure out how big the lots are. There's either going to be sixteen castles with room for a few serfs or two hundred and thirty huts with a hog wallow."

"This has been our place since we were kids."

"Honey, if it's your childhood you're worried about, I've got about a thousand pictures of you in war paint, brandishing a bow and arrow. And another fifty of Larry squatting by a fire, stirring imaginary maize in an imaginary pot."

"You know, we should do something. What if we burned the Volvo? What if we burned all our stuff?"

"Arson's always fun."

"Hey, you want to hang out at Larry's in a little bit? Maybe twenty minutes? I gotta meet Mary Ann, but—"

"You're not inviting her to your birthday party, are you?"

My dad's a butcher, and I am, too, kind of. I know knives. And that question of Teresa's has got an edge on it.

"I mean, do that," she says, "and your mom'd start speaking in tongues."

"I'm just gonna talk to her, then hook up with you guys."

"I'd watch your step with Mary Ann if I were you. I was surfing the Net the other night, and I'm pretty sure I saw her on that Naked Nurses Who Kill for Kicks site. She was the one with the deadly bedpan."

"Very funny. See you in a little bit."

I'm not like Larry and Teresa. I have to do stuff. I can't just sit like that naked guy with his chin on his fist and think. So I go look in the Volvo (okay, it's just barely a Volvo now, but it used to be), and there's Larry's Oreos and Teresa's dictionary and my portable radio so I can get the games from U of I.

I grab some kindling and logs out from under the tarp and build a fire right where we always do. It starts slow and smoky at the bottom, then speeds up. I'd like to build fires for a living.

I take off my down vest, roll up my sleeves, and start chopping wood. I'm good at that, too. I've got a sharp ax and a wedge. I'm strong for a point guard. Lean and mean. I show that old log no mercy.

"Hey, woodsman!"

I'm panting and sweaty. My heart is going *boom-da-boom*. My lungs feel big and clean. I don't want to stop, so I don't for a minute. Then I say it: "Hi, Mary Ann."

"Cool fire."

I lay the ax on my vest because I don't want to forget it when I leave. "Do you believe what they're doing to this place?" I point. "That old Volvo used to be a stagecoach and a spaceship—"

"It's a wreck now."

Mary Ann took that stud out of her tongue for Christmas, but she's still a little punked out in her tiny skirt, Doc Martens, ripped stockings (not the smooth dressed-up-for-church kind but the rough stripper kind), and, naturally, purple-and-green hair.

She asks, "Want to smoke?"

I tell her, "Maybe one little hit wouldn't hurt."

She carries joints in a flat tin box with a jaguar on the top. I watch her choose one, going kind of eenie-meenie-minie-moe. She lights up, takes a huge lungful, settles down in one of the broken-down chairs, passes me the spliff.

The dope really helps. Inside of thirty seconds, those piercings in her eyebrows kind of shimmer and her long earrings look like tinsel.

I tell her, "I was shooting hoops about half an hour ago, and I swear to god I could not miss. I've been in the zone before but not like that. Have you ever felt like you could do no wrong?"

Her knees are kind of chapped from the cold weather, and there's a scab on the left one, like when we were seven, everybody got skates for Christmas, and she kept falling down.

She doesn't look at me when she says, "I just got another D in pharmacology. I could flunk out of community college. How pathetic is that?"

"How many exams are there?"

"All semester? Like, five, probably."

"Did you study or was it just really hard?"

Mary Ann can be pretty, but she's not now. "What do you know about trying hard?"

"Hey, I try."

She shakes her head. "Bullshit. Teresa and Larry help you with everything."

"We study together is all. Why don't you do that?"

She exhales my way. "I don't get along with my classmates, okay? They're, like, intense. They never want to party or do anything except look through a microscope. And they dress weird."

I can't help it. I start to laugh. She's mad for about four seconds, then she does, too. Partly it's the weed, partly it's just funny.

"Sorry," she says finally, "about what I said. I know you study. I'm just jealous or something." She flounces her little skirt. "I need a new look. I need a new life. Everybody loves my mom at the hospital, okay? She is, like, you know, Super Nurse. So of course I'm supposed to ace everything, get my cap, and go to work right beside her." She doesn't want to exhale, so her voice is kind of squeaky. "That's a lot of pressure."

I nod. "Yeah, my mom, too. High standards and all that."

"No kidding. And then there's, you know, these guys I run with, and all they talk about is how empty materialism is, but one of them's got a two-hundred-dollar Marilyn Manson wristwatch. Is that some kind of irony I don't get, or is it just stupid?"

I shrug. "Sounds stupid to me."

She leans toward the fire like people do. She just wants to get warm, but with her hands out like that, it looks like she's trying to push something back. She asks, "When that old car was a spaceship, where were you going?"

"The planet Ampara—this place Larry made up. All kinds of stuff to eat, sunshine all the time, no parents, and if you got bored you just reorganized your cells and were somebody else for a while."

She grins. "I should do that. I should reorganize my cells into somebody who studies."

"You got good grades last year when you were a senior."

"They were all right. I hated my mom, so they couldn't be too good or she'd, you know, be proud of me. And we couldn't have that, could we."

"Do what you said and study. You'll be fine."

She's looking at me a different way now, and she's pretty again. "You think?"

"Yeah."

She moves toward me. "Want to make out?"

We put our arms around each other's waists and head for the Volvo.

She slips one hand under my flannel shirt. "How many sit-ups do you do, anyway?"

"A thousand or so a day."

"Get out."

"Really. Larry counts for me."

"Must be the high point of his day."

I hold the door for her, then hustle around to the other side. I'm barely in before she kisses me. Or maybe it's I'm barcly in before I kiss her. Either way, it's hot.

She pulls away first and pants like she's been running. "I don't know how far I want to go today."

I slide away from her, lean against the door. "So should we stop?"

She puts one hand on the back of the seat, one on the steering wheel. She looms over me. "Hey, I didn't say that."

TERESA

Is it all my mother's fault? Months from now, when the locals gossip about me at Kroger's, will they say she's the reason I graduated on Thursday and ran away with two boys on Friday?

Who knows, and who cares? I just slip into my hundred-dollar Adidas and get ready to run.

But before I can even open the door, Elliot calls from the pasture and says the site of our childhood is in jeopardy. *And* I have to listen to some nonsense about how Mary Ann "just wants to talk."

After that I'm more than glad to lace up my trainers and jog up Erie Street, onto Big Bend, past the Dairy Delight, past the single moms smoking and waiting for a bus, past the we-love-Jesus-more-than-you-do Baptist church, the Horseshoe Bar & Grill, Bob's Handsome Fruits and Vegetables (Where did he get that adjective?), around the Teen Canteen (leftover hormones still stinking the place up), then beside the dress factory/sweatshop. I say hi to Mrs. Twitchell, who's walking her stupid dachshund (King, no less), and sprint by the new Rite Aid. (I still miss Toon's Sundries.) I wave to the cops (I know them all by name— that's the kind of sprawling metropolis Wendleville is), lope past some more churches, take a sharp right at the bank, head down Summit and through the new subdivision (The Pines @ Wendleville), where somebody is almost always playing the same pathetic Cheap Trick album. Then out toward Wendleville Memorial, with its famous ER.

There used to be nothing but a dirt road out there, and once a few years ago an honest-to-god fawn waltzed out of the walnut trees and ran beside me for three hundred yards or so. I thought that was a sign. Maybe my mother would die in a fire like Bambi's mother? I could only hope.

I finish my run, take a shower, manage to eat a banana, grab a camera, and stroll out the door.

At the corner I wait for some cars to go by, then a Jeep full of kids who wave like I was their long-lost friend.

I know those guys. I've been in school with them all my life. I've been on student council, treasurer of the Drama Club, and helped decorate the cafeteria for a dance. (I wanted the theme to be Revenge; they chose Boogie Nights.) So I'm part of that world. Just not a big part. Larry and Elliot—they're pretty much my whole world.

When I cut down the alley, Mr. Ornstein waves at me as he tugs at his cellar doors. I watch them open like a book. I watch him disappear into the dark, another goddamned underground man like my dad. Another useless bastard sawing and sanding, gluing and clamping and fixing. Another tinkerer. Another handyman. Another complete nutcase.

Larry's back door is open. His dad uses the mud porch for boots and jackets. He's a doctor; he can afford a really nice house, but Doc Cooperman would rather spend his money on decoys and ammo.

I stop long enough to take a picture of some Red Wing boots with a lot of blood on them.

I'm using the old Polaroid. It isn't as slick as my Nikon Coolpix 5700, but I still like that whir when the film slides out, the wave to get the snapshot dry, the way things come to the surface. All kinds of stuff, actually, floating up from who-knows-where.

So I take another shot of those gory boots. I don't have many of Doc because he's like Bigfoot—always shambling off into the trees.

I once asked Larry what was up with his father. He said, "Doc likes to sleep by himself on the ground."

Isn't that all you need to know about the guy? And speaking of all you need to know: Larry never calls his father anything but Doc. And he calls his mother, whose real name is Esther, Madame Zora.

There are a lot of things that make Larry and me love each other, and one of those things is how screwed up our parents are.

Jesus, I sound like Elliot. Digressing Elliot. Gorgeous Elliot.

I kind of tiptoe through Larry's kitchen because the silver Audi parked outside means his mom has a client. Sure enough—there they are in the den.

Someone (Why is it always a woman? Don't men want to know the future?) sits with her back to me, so I keep my mouth shut. A lot of Zora's clients don't want anybody to know what they're up to. You ought to see them hustle to their cars in sunglasses and shawls like gangsters' wives.

Larry's mother gives me a little I-know-you're-there smile, then reaches for her client's hand and holds it in both of hers.

She warms to her work, and I mean that literally. I've had my chronically chilly mitts in her cozy ones. I've actually asked her if my mother ever loved me, but all I got was some b.s. about toxic karmic connections.

I raise my camera. I want a shot with just an arm or shoulder; otherwise the only thing I'm interested in is the light on the couch, on the sugarcane pattern of the drapes, on the stupid ceramic pineapple by the TV.

Larry's mother used to redecorate every year: Chinese, Desert Southwest, Cape Cod. She used to play golf and bridge. Drank a little too much. Had a boyfriend.

And then came that day on the thirteenth tee. The storm out of the west. The lightning. The gift.

I watch a photo develop, then almost can't hear the next question because this time Mrs. Incognito pretty much whispers in Zora's ear. It's kind of romantic. Not sexy, just superclose.

I wave good-bye but don't leave. Once I'm gone, Larry's mom will be different. And her customer. And the light. Especially the light. I wait for the gardener to power by and hide the click of my Polaroid, then take more pictures.

I climb the stairs to Larry's bedroom and peek in. He holds the classic index finger to lips (*"Shhh!"*), waves me in, and hisses, "I'm watching *Passion Fish*."

LARRY

I'm not just *watching* the movie *Passion Fish;* I'm *in* the movie *Passion Fish.* Mary McDonnell is the bitter paraplegic, a "bitch on wheels." Alfre Woodard is her just-out-of-rehab companion. David Strathairn in tight jeans and white rubber boots plays an unhappily married local fisherman.

I'm the physical therapist. Better than the one in the film, much better. Kinder. More understanding. With real healing hands.

I often insinuate myself into movies because that way I can change the ending. Why should Mary fall in love with David? Maybe Mary and Alfre should look deep into each other's eyes, then get on Amazon for the complete works of Sappho. Maybe David and I should go fishing.

Anything, frankly, but what everybody expects.

When I go to the Petite Four Cinemas at the edge of town, I walk out about halfway through and smoke. Or if I'm with my friends, I bring a book and sit bathed in neon while the corn sways and rasps not twenty yards away. I prefer things at the midpoint. The inevitable doesn't hold my interest very long.

If I had my way, films would run about forty-two minutes. Then the lights should go up and those in attendance could suggest satisfying finales: You who want Mary and David to get together should stand over there. Those who want an alligator to eat David may sit by me.

Elliot, Teresa, and I are in the first twenty minutes of our movie. The plan is to leave Wendleville immediately after graduation. Once we're established on the West Coast, we may only have friends who are willing to play not just second fiddle but fourth violin. A single nay from any of us, and the candidate is cast out of the Garden of Eden. Our Garden of Eden. We won't need an angel with a fiery sword to keep them out, either. I'll just stand there. Flaming.

What twists and turns, I wonder, will this plot take? How many alternate endings are there?

When Teresa shows up, I get to turn off the TV at just the right time.

She waves some papers. "Don't let me forget to give Elliot his *Gatsby* essay."

"How is it?"

"Wanders all over the place, but the grammar's right. Now, anyway."

She goes to the south window and looks out. From there she can see a victory garden (our most senior citizen still calls it that), Boots the yard dog, and the two Holsteins Mr. Tieman likes to milk.

"Don't tell Elliot I said this, but it is kind of a shame about the pasture. Where we're going it's all neon and tall buildings."

"Did he tell you he was down there with Mary Ann?"

"How," Teresa asks, "can he kiss her? Milk runs out of her nose."

"Once," I remind her. "When she was thirteen."

"Still, you never know. I wouldn't want to chance it."

I can't help but point out, "And it was milk and chocolate pudding."

Teresa shudders. "Even worse."

"You, however, can let as much milk and pudding run out of your nose as you want, since, as Elliot continues to point out, he likes you as a friend."

"Bite me, Larry."

I pick up her hand, put it in my mouth. Sideways. I press down just hard enough. I can taste the soap she uses. Dove.

"I meant figuratively." She pulls her hand away, wipes it on her thigh. Her legs are long and brown. Muscled and downy. Actually, very downy. So downy

that she should shave. But her legs are still her best feature. She wears shorts all year round; today's—beneath
her North Face jacket—are lime green.

Teresa steps into my arms. She's tall, so I let my
head rest on her bony shoulder. She flinches and asks,
"What's on your hair, Moose?"

Is she not a clever girl? "For your information, this
particular mousse is formulated to give long-lasting
control, body, and sheen."

She gives me a sisterly kiss. "What," she asks, "do
you want to do when Elliot gets here?"

"Let's practice being happy so we know how to act
when we get to California."

2

. . . that dark glacier you woke with.

ELLIOT

Mary Ann left a message on my voice mail. She got a B on her anatomy test. I haven't really talked to her since our assignation (any big words I know are thanks to Larry and Teresa) in the pasture a couple of weeks ago, but that's how we are. We just see each other. And, anyway, she's not the kind of girl a guy gets serious about.

I want to smoke a joint, but there's no telling when my mom'll appear and want to vacuum or pick up some dirty clothes. She's already talking about how clean the house has to be for my party, and that's a month away. I've got, like, no privacy at all, but if I complain she says this might be *my* room but it's *her* house.

Speaking of which, Teresa's mother took off because she wanted "a room of her own." I guess there's this famous book that says every woman needs one, so Rita (that's Teresa's mother's name) went to get hers. She stomped downstairs one morning, told Teresa's dad, "I'll take my meds, but I won't stay here with you and get quaint." And she told Teresa, "I don't like my life and I don't like my husband. I realize you may never understand or forgive me."

(I know that story by heart because Teresa tells it about every twenty minutes.)

My mother still prays for Rita. My mother prays for a lot of people. When she really gets into it (praying, I mean), she lies down on the floor and stretches out her arms. It looks like she tried to fly off the dining room table and didn't make cruising altitude. Why that's better than kneeling is beyond me, but every now and then I'll come home from school or basketball practice or the pasture and there she'll be, mumbling into the carpet.

My mom is strict: three meals a day, cloth napkins every time, sit up straight, no elbows on the table, and don't talk with your mouth full.

But not Teresa's mom. She had stacks of paper everywhere, all kinds of books facedown (which drives my mother crazy because it breaks their spines), and people eating whenever and maybe standing up. But every now and then, Teresa would come home from school and the house would be perfect. And no more Chef Boyardee or those tired bags o' salad. No way. It'd be candles and roses and filet mignon from my dad's shop, plus promises from Rita about how she was going to be a good wife and mother. "Like Elliot's."

But Teresa never bought it. She knew in a day or two, Rita would get a new idea for some lame novel or story or poem and it'd be business as usual.

What Teresa's mom was, though, was great-looking. She probably still is. Beautiful, I mean. Red hair, white skin, green eyes, perfect teeth—the whole package. (Teresa could be pretty if she wasn't so skinny, but Larry says she's got something called food issues and those come from her mom blowing her off a few years ago. I guess. Maybe. All I know is show me a malt and a burger, turn your back for a second, and they're gone.)

Anyway, I'll never forget this one day I was waiting in the kitchen for Teresa to come down. Everything was shipshape (at least for Rita it was). There was this picture of Paris on the wall: busy street, guy in a striped shirt, people sitting around having coffee, saying *"Oui, oui."*

By the way, when we're loaded, Larry and Teresa and I talk about Europe right after graduation instead of California. Larry speaks something like three languages already, so he could order food and find us a place to stay. And I can get a job anywhere cutting meat. French cows are probably built just like American ones. Except for the berets. Ha-ha.

I really don't want to stay in Wendleville and have babies so my mom can dress them up and show off at church. So if my best friends want to go to Europe, then Europe it is.

But I digress. Guess how many times I've heard that from schoolteachers? Along with the usual C.

Well, only in class. I'm an A+ on the basketball court. And girls are always saying I'm the cutest boy in Wendleville. (My mom claims my good looks are a gift from God and I should use them for His glory. Don't you wonder what that is? And don't you know how fooling around with girls isn't it?)

Sorry. Back to Rita's kitchen. So I was waiting for Teresa, and her mom was writing away (she called it *composing*) in a fuzzy robe with a T-shirt under it. Her left hand all tangled in her hair. Scribble, scribble, scribble, and at top speed, too.

Then out of nowhere she looked up and said, "You'll know what I mean by this, Elliot, because you're attractive. Nobody takes you seriously, do they?"

I was just about to say I sure knew what she was talking about because girls think all I am is cute, but she wasn't finished. She took a sip of coffee and said, "Yet we understand things other people don't."

Then she forgot all about me and started scribbling away again.

But what she said turned out to be true. When she left town, everybody else was, "Oh my god." And "How could she abandon her family?" Well, I understood totally. Wasn't that what Larry and Teresa and I were going to do—run away from home and get rooms of our own together?

TERESA

It's way too early to actually pack for California (Larry says only two suitcases each), but I like thinking about getting out of here, so I sit on my bed and wonder which photographs to take along.

Digital cameras make art easy. I plug things in, hit a few buttons, look at my computer, then print whatever I want. The keepers. Not what you'd think, either. And for sure not the pretty ones.

I like to just stick the camera out a car window, or hold it way up over my head so there's no way to compose the shot. I'm random's biggest fan.

I like bad photography in general: Give me an out-of-focus leer; a telephone pole jutting out of somebody's noggin; four bozos in coats with their heads cut off; close-ups of some body part—a crease in the neck, maybe, a bulging vein, nose without end. Amen.

I like men clotted at street corners, and people at the bus stop losing their grip. I like moms who treat their kids like hostile witnesses. I like numbed-up teenagers with their CD players, the bass drowning out their mamas' nonsense.

And doesn't just the word *mama* bring back memories. When I was thirteen and mine got weird on me, I'd call Larry and Elliot. They'd drop what they were doing and meet me up at Toon's because Larry's solution to everything was a candy bar. My friends always settled me down, made me feel better. They still do.

Sometimes we'd coast by Holy Family afterward because I was already working on a whole bunch of photographs of girls going into church. (Two years ago I showed them at the Apex Gallery in Springfield.)

I liked taking those pictures. The guys would lounge around on the warm concrete. Larry read, Elliot was sexy even then. Older girls would show up, fresh out of their boyfriends' cars some of them, looking scared or snotty or guilty or bored, and on their way up the steps, they'd get a load of Elliot and stop dead in their tracks. I could almost hear the cornball lyrics playing in the Top 40 of their stupid hearts: "If only he were mine, life would be so fine—*blah, blah, blah.*"

I'll bet my dad felt that way about Mom once. Well, look how that turned out: canned spaghetti and her up at all hours wired on Folgers, pretending to be Sylvia Plath. Did I mention she used a quill and bottles of ink? Oh yeah. I'd come down for breakfast and there she'd be, heat coming off her like a burning bush. Or asleep with her head on the fancy paper she had to have, so that when I woke her up the last sentence was tattooed across one cheek: the illustrated mom.

I've got a picture of that. She could wander into a gallery someday and see it. So what? I don't need her. I don't need anybody but Larry and Elliot.

We figure at least three thousand dollars each—enough to get us where we're going, pay first and last month's rent, and buy us some time to find jobs. When I worked at the outlet mall between here and Spring-field the last two summers and Christmas vacations, I told my dad—like he cared, anyway—that I was saving for a car. Actually, I was saving for my life.

LARRY

Teresa must have been going through photographs, because we just spent an hour on the phone talking about her mother. Again.

I always thought Rita was silly and delusional, and I imagine she still is, living somewhere in half a duplex of her own. But I used to like sitting in her disaster of a kitchen, waiting for Teresa and talking about mortality and movies.

It haunted her that the Cary Grant of *Blonde Venus* was no longer the Cary Grant of *Indiscreet*. And the Harrison Ford of *American Graffiti* (playing the hot-rodder Bob Falfa, for you trivia fans) was stunning while the Harrison Ford of *Witness* was merely handsome.

She liked to stare at some perfectly awful rendition of Paris that she bought at the mall in Springfield, ca-ress her alabaster skin, and put herself into that print:

There she was on the Rive Gauche, chatting with other writers, sought after and appreciated. No hormonal husband to deal with, no needy daughter.

She liked to query Elliot about the dilemma of the beautiful thus misunderstood. From me she wanted only insight and understanding, as if I, like my mother, had been struck by lightning and could suddenly detect dark energy in the etheric body and find lost pets.

Coincidentally, I saw Rita almost at the moment of my own transmogrification. (Such a harsh word. Why not *transformation*? Or am I the kind of bitter fag who spares no one, least of all himself?)

I'm talking about that memorable afternoon five years ago in Toon's—a little hole-in-the-wall store that sold lottery tickets, tobacco, ammunition, and magazines. I was supposed to be shopping for Elliot's birthday, but I was staring at the cover of the April *Playboy* instead. Rita came in for a Coke. We nodded, said hi; she wafted away with her expensive haiku notebook, leaving in her wake half a dozen dazzled men.

Then I strolled to the comic book rack and picked up a new Teen Titans: page after page of swollen biceps and muscular haunches. The earth, as in Hemingway, moved.

I had a very bad moment, clutching my suddenly suspicious Butterfinger.

I was never a hysterical person, so I was certainly not about to run screaming out of the store and start cooking ginger-encrusted tuna for a roomful of florists.

Nor was I about to turn with trembling fingers the pages of the nearest phone book until I found *Therapists.*

First I paid for my candy bar, then I looked again at the nearly naked beauties clothed in tantalizing scraps on the cover of *Playboy.*

I knew they were everything that a real man was supposed to want. What did I feel? Certainly admiration for the obvious good shape they were in, because Elliot and I had just begun to lift weights in his garage.

But nothing like the woozy, wonderfully sleazy, sky-splintering, everything-tumbling-down-around-me sensations that hit when one of the Titans leaned over to defuse a nuclear device.

Oh, Jesus. I knew what happened to boys like me in a town like Wendleville.

Riding home, weaving drunkenly on my trusty bicycle, I looked at the world through new eyes. New, possibly gay eyes.

On the one hand, the wrought-iron railing leading the elderly into the library still resembled an enormous licorice. I recognized every leggy dandelion in every neglected lawn. Officer Wilson, giving somebody a parking ticket, waved to me. And King, the Twitchells' dachshund, made his usual halfhearted lunge at my tires.

But what if I was what I feared and everyone found out? Would stout and ducktailed Ms. Wilcox take away my library card or with a conspiratorial wink steer me right to the Hardy Boys? Would the dandelions hang their yellow heads in shame and disappointment? How about you, Officer Wilson—am I now suspected of everything? And King—would you never turn your very long back on me again?

I rode to Teresa's. She was mowing the lawn in red pedal pushers, blue Keds, and a white T-shirt from the Gap. Usually I would have offered a dozen jokes about patriotism, color coordination, and the Protestant work ethic, but all I could do was stand there. I was thirteen, but I can still feel the clammy shirt (the green one, of all things) clinging to the small of my back.

"Larry," she asked, "what's wrong?"

"Oh god," I squeaked. "I might be as queer as a three-dollar bill."

3

. . . every certainty I thought I knew.

ELLIOT

It's not even April. The University of Illinois at Urbana-Champaign is only a couple hundred miles from here, but Mom's already worried about me going away to school. If she knew that Larry and Teresa and I are heading straight for California right after graduation, she'd have a heart attack.

She wants me out from under her feet this morning, but she's nice about it. Makes up some errands for me to run, gives me twenty bucks, and says, "Whatever's left over is yours." Because that's what she always said when I was little. It was her way of getting around Dad, who wanted me to work for every penny "so I'd know the value of money." *Blah, blah, blah.*

But first she asks me to help her get some bedclothes off the line. She could have somebody from Merry Maids come in, like Aunt Stephanie does. Or pay to have everything done by Black & White Cleaners uptown, which is almost right next door to Dad's store—Madison's Designer Meats. But she says she likes being a stay-at-home mom.

I guess. She is one, that's for sure. And a really good one. Dad likes a clean house and a meal on the table when he comes home from work, and Ephesians 5:22 says: "Wives, submit to your husbands as to the Lord." So there's that.

What if she had never heard of Ephesians? She'd be different, right? Not the mom I know at all. But another kind. A trashy mom maybe. Who fooled around. Man, I can't get my mind around that.

Larry and Teresa and I talk all the time about deep stuff: Who would we be if we weren't us? Would we still be friends? What if Rita was my mom? Would I be all bitter like Teresa, or would I try to find her and work things out? What if Larry'd been kidnapped by Englishmen when he was, like, two seconds old? He'd have an accent, eat "chips" instead of fries, and be named Nigel.

If I didn't know Larry and Teresa, who would tell me not to worry so much about what the Bible says? Who'd remind me it was written in something called Aramaic, and that was turned into Greek, which was turned into another version ("*Version,* Elliot. Not the truth, but a version!") by old King James.

He's a smart guy, Larry is. And he and Teresa mean well. But let's face it: The Bible is the Bible. And it says husbands should love their wives like their own bodies, and he who loves his wife loves himself because nobody ever hated his own flesh but nourished it and cherished it.

I nourish my flesh three times a day and take it to the gym, but I hate it sometimes. It gets me into all kinds of trouble.

Anyway, I'm out in the yard thinking stuff like this when a flatbed truck goes by hauling one of those big yellow Caterpillar tractors.

Mom drops her blue laundry basket. "Some people like change," she says, sounding all kind of wistful. "But I don't." She pats me in that way she has. "It's not going to be the same around here without that pasture."

She steps out of her shoes then (the lawn is still kind of brown, but it's warm out and bright), so I kick off my Adidas. She goes to the other side of a sheet, I stay put. And the way the sun is, all I can see is her shadow, okay? So I've got a clothespin or two off when I hear her say, "Who am I, Elliot?" And she does this thing she hasn't done in years. This one-arm-up-and-one-arm-back-hands-bent-at-the-wrist-Steve-Martin-walk-like-an-Egyptian thing. She's still got all the moves that just put me away when I was little.

Then she comes back the other way. This time she's got her head back and both arms out, and her shadow is kind of gliding. I yell, "Bride of Frankenstein!" Next, one shoulder is all hunched up and one arm is dangling, so I shout, "Igor!" Because years and years ago she and

I used to watch *Fright Night* or *Creature Feature* on TV
and eat about twenty tons of popcorn.

So I'm falling down laughing by this time, okay? I
mean, I'm on the grass trying to pull myself together
when it hits me—pretty much for the first time—how
much she's going to miss me. That's the change she was
talking about. Not just the pasture.

It's like she reads my mind, because all of a sudden
she says, "Well, enough silliness for today. What will the
neighbors think?" So I get up and brush myself off.

We don't say anything, but we work like a team:
I fold, she tugs; I go left, she goes right. It's like a little
dance. We end up looking right at each other, our arms
out as far as they can go, the last sheet between us.

"Thank you," she says, stepping back into her
shoes. "That was fun."

Then she walks me toward the driveway. Opens the
car door for me. Like a valet. She watches me settle in.

"Put your seat belt on."

I don't want to, but I do. Then I start the Mustang
and listen to it rumble. She motions for me to shut it
down.

"Honey," she says, "are you seeing enough of your
other friends?"

This again. "Besides Larry and Teresa."

She picks a piece of lint off my sweatshirt. "*In addi-
tion to* is what I was thinking."

"They're my best friends."

"But not your only friends. I miss having your teammates drop by."

"Mom, when the season's over, I'm over."

"Oh, I'm sure that's not true."

"It sure is. Larry and Teresa don't care if I win the game or not; they like me anyway. If I broke my leg, you know who'd come and see me in the hospital? Larry and Teresa. And if I got gangrene and my leg fell off, you know who'd push me around in a wheelchair? Larry and Teresa."

"I'd just like you," my mother says, "to be around a variety of young people."

I want to say, *What's the use? I'm out of here the second I graduate.* But I settle for this: "You don't like me being around Mary Ann."

Mom straightens up. "Well-dressed young people."

"Larry's well-dressed."

"Larry's—"

I watch her jaw go tight. She's looking for the right words, the ones that'll say exactly what she wants but not tick me off. Here they come.

"Larry," she says, "is misguided and confused."

"You know how you always say God doesn't make mistakes? Well, He made Larry, didn't He?"

She takes half a step back. "I'm sure he told you to say that."

"Why? Because I'm not smart enough to think of it myself?" I start the car again. "Thanks a lot."

I wasn't lying. Larry didn't tell me to say that. Teresa did. But at least I remembered it. Now I really don't want to do Mom's stupid errands, so I cruise by the high school. I've got this cool Black Cat exhaust system on the Ford. So everybody knows it's me. Larry says it's like the trumpeters in the old days who let the whole town know the king was coming.

When I pull up, the courts are empty except for one pickup game. Billy Field and Drew Pearson versus a couple of guys Mary Ann probably knows but are in my class: Carl Thomas and Wayne Beeder. They're what Larry calls boutique anarchists because they buy their dog collars and boots with Daddy's credit card.

Drew is a mouth-breather who hates anyone Billy tells him to. Billy is just long stringy hair, bad teeth, and tattoos. They're both D's in English, D's in everything except gym and wood shop.

Billy's truck is parked right at the edge of the grass. Both doors are open. The radio's turned all the way up, like guys will do.

That's fun when it's something like that Freddy Mercury cut about being champions of the world. But this is rap, which Larry describes as "fears approaching on horseback." I'm not exactly sure what that means, but it sure nails this stuff.

The truck is shaking and belching smoke from both ends. When I lean in and turn the key, I can't help but see that the padding on the dash and doors is gone.

The clock's wires just hang there. The whole cockpit looks like it's been home to about three wolverines.

"Hey! What do you think you're doin'?"

I walk toward Billy and the others. "That carburetor's set way too rich, man. You're wasting gas."

"You let me worry about my carburetor, okay?"

"Can I get winners?" I ask.

"Come on and play," says Carl. "You and somebody against the rest of us."

"Fuck that," Billy says. "He'll just win."

Carl shrugs. "Be on his side."

"Fuck him."

I say that I'll take Drew.

Billy shakes his head. "We were here first, hotshot. You've already got a Mustang and all the girls in the world. You can't have everything."

I hold up both hands like you do to show there's no problem.

Then he changes his mind. "Okay. Take Drew. But first I gotta pee." Billy jogs to the far end of the court. There really isn't anybody else around. He at least faces the track and the soccer field. It's still gross.

Carl wanders over. "Class act, huh?"

"No kidding."

"Going to U of I this fall?"

"Yes," I lie.

"I got in, too. I'm thinking of pledging."

When I don't say anything, he adds, "A fraternity."

"Oh yeah. I don't know yet."

"The Phi Delts are all jocks; they'd kill to get you. I'm looking for a house with a bunch of math majors. Is Larry going out of state? Stanford or something?"

"Probably." Which I hope counts as just half a lie.

"He'll be a lot happier in college. He's such a fish out of water in this place."

All of a sudden Carl isn't just somebody in a Black Sabbath T-shirt who sat behind me in math. He's an okay guy. If I was actually going to U of I, I could see hanging out with him. We could go for coffee, pile our books up on a table, look out a window at those ivy walls, and say how different college is from high school.

Then Billy jogs back. "When you two are finished making out, we can play."

I stroll over to Drew, throw one arm over his shoulder, and whisper, "They're going to be all over me. You just drift under the basket all innocent-like, and I'll get you the ball. Heads up, okay?"

Just like I said: Wayne tries some D, but he's totally outclassed. Carl's clumsy in his stupid boots that must take a week to lace up.

I drain two or three from downtown, and when somebody comes out past the paint to get me, I pass to Drew.

"Eight–zip."

"You faggot," Billy says, walking toward the sidelines. He's playing in overalls and cheap kicks from Big 5.

Two seconds later I steal the ball and bounce one

between Carl's legs to Drew, who scores again. Which just lights the kid up. I wonder if he's ever made a basket before in his life.

"Where's your faggot friend, faggot?" asks Billy. I just hold the ball curled into my forearm like it's the head of my enemy.

I tell him, "Probably studying. That's why he's a thousand times smarter than you are."

"You should know, man. He's your boyfriend."

I rocket the ball right at him two-handed and he charges.

I sidestep and down he goes. I'm on him like a cat. I punch him a couple of times and he just covers up. Everybody knows my dad showed me about thirty ways to kill somebody with my thumb. So Billy doesn't move. I tell him, "You just forget about Larry."

"Fuck you."

I stand up, shake hands with Carl, and tap Drew's fist with mine. I say "Good game" and head for my car. But slow. Like there's no hurry. Like I don't care whether Billy gets up or not. I don't turn around, but I hear Carl say good-bye, too.

His Jeep, a nice fat-wheeled Wrangler, is parked beside my Mustang. He gets in, rattles the stick shift, then says, "Tell Larry to stay awake, okay? He's all Billy talks about. He's obsessed with the guy."

I do Mom's errands. I go to Kroger's, and people there know me and say how great it was that I'd won the big game. Again. But I'm still thinking about that idiot Billy.

I'm supposed to pick up some pork chops for dinner, so I stop by the shop. Dad's busy; I throw on an apron and help out, glad to think about something else.

A lot of it's just some-of-this and some-of-that, please, but it's like a game to me. Another game I'm good at. I can hit a pound of hamburger right on the button five times out of ten, and I never miss by more than an ounce or two.

I know some people think being a butcher is gross, but to me it's not. I don't slam stuff around like it wasn't alive once. We only sell raised-on-the-ground, no-hormones chickens. I love those little guys. *Gals,* actually. Hens. I like to see them in the case all cozy with their neighbors. I like to hold one up and show a customer. And if I cut one up for somebody, I use the sharpest knife and pretend I'm a samurai. They come apart like they want to. They're putty in my hands.

When business slows down, Dad and I wash up together, eat some saltines and bologna. People go by wearing jackets (it's March, it's cloudy, so it's still Crock-Pot weather), but inside where we are it's just right.

Dad points. "What happened to your hand?"

"Got in a fight."

"Who with?"

"Billy Field."

"That psycho. What was it about?"

"Larry mostly."

He starts to sharpen one of his Wüsthof trimmers. "Larry's smart, so—"

"All A's."

Dad just keeps sharpening, but he doesn't like it that I interrupted him. "So he must know what he's doing if he wants to live that gay life."

I make myself another little sandwich. "Teresa says it's not like guys who are that way want to be that way. They're born—"

"Is he going to U of I?"

"No."

My dad says, "Good."

He motions for the mustard, and I hand it to him. "I thought you liked Larry."

He doesn't look at me. He just takes his time picking the perfect cracker. "He works out in my garage. He eats at my table. He's my son's best friend."

"But . . . ?"

He leans over and flicks a piece of sawdust off his boot. His red-and-black Tony Lamas. Which he wears to look taller. "I didn't go to college, you know that. My country needed me, so I went in the service. There was a guy like Larry in boot camp. Everybody liked him; nobody trusted him."

Outside somebody knocks on the window and waves. Dad grins and waves back. Life in a small town. The kind of thing that drives Larry and Teresa crazy.

My dad cuts another piece of bologna and offers it to me, but I shake my head. "You're a heartbeat away from being eighteen, son. You'll get an education, get married, and before you know it, have kids of your own. You're going to want the best for them, just like I want the best for you."

"I can't believe all of a sudden you don't like Larry."

He wipes off the boning knife and shears. "Is Teresa going to U of I?"

"What? No."

"Good. When you go to college, it's time for a clean break."

Just then somebody comes into the shop. He says to her, "Be right with you." To me it's "You're a man now, all right? Think for yourself." Not mean, though. He's not ragging on me.

Then he hugs me. It's quick, but he does it. I'm standing there all confused. I kind of want to call Larry; wait—not Larry. What would I tell him? "My dad says I can't trust you." Teresa then. Except I know what she'd say, which is pretty much what she always says about my dad: "How can you take him seriously? He's forty-two years old, drives a red Pontiac Firebird, and won't let anybody cut his hair but some fairy in a strip mall."

Maybe I'll just work this one out for myself.

TERESA

We were barely thirteen when Larry told me he might be gay.

I was mowing the lawn. My mother was out with her goofy poetry notebook; Dad was at work, probably driving the forklift that would end up falling over on him so he could get a big fat settlement, stay home all day, and make my mother nuttier than she already was.

I got Larry inside so he could go to pieces in private. He just sat at the kitchen table and sobbed. I'd never seen him—I'd probably never seen anybody—cry like that.

I held his hand; I put my arms around him; I got a Dr Pepper from the fridge and made him drink a little. Finally I asked him, "What happened?"

He mumbled something about a comic book.

I said, "A comic book made you gay?"

"It was Teen Titans," he wailed.

"So? Elliot reads Teen Titans."

"Not," he sobbed, "like I do." And he started in again.

I knew that Larry and I in the backseat of the Volvo were different from Elliot and anybody in the front seat. They were all over each other; we pecked like little birds in the snow.

So did that mean he was gay, or were we just sort of low voltage?

"You know, this could be all my fault."

He shook his head. "It's not your fault. You didn't get a boner from Teen Titans."

"Look, Mary Ann told me stuff that girls can do. You go home; I'll take a shower, and then I'll come over."

He eyed me suspiciously. "Doesn't it just make you sick to your stomach? It just makes me sick to my stomach."

"What does?"

"Being queer."

I put my arms around him again. "Shut up." I pushed him toward the door. "Now get out of here. I'll be at your house before you know it."

When I got there, Doc wasn't home; Esther's note said something about an early tee time. I stood in the kitchen just about radioactive with lip gloss and reeking of Pur Désir, a Christmas present from my pathetic father.

Upstairs, Larry was staring at *The Last of the Mohicans.* I could tell he'd been crying again. I waited until "Hawkeye" had saved Cora.

"Are you okay?"

"Listen," he said, wiping his eyes. "I just looked up *homosexuality* on the Internet. One in every ten men is gay, okay? One in ten."

"So?"

"So there are twenty-six thousand people in Wendleville. Let's say half of those are guys. That's thirteen thousand. Where are the thirteen hundred queers?"

Larry always had curly copper-colored hair and round cheeks with built-in march-of-the-wooden-soldier spots of color on each one. Those spots were positively on fire.

"Well," I said, "there's that guy who cuts hair at the Mane Attraction."

"With the eye shadow and the Chihuahua? Oh, Jesus. I'm not like that, and I'm not like Mr. Quentin. Where's the other twelve hundred and ninety-eight?"

"Mr. Quentin is gay?"

"Are you kidding? Did you ever see him walk? He's forty years old and he's got a roommate. And they both wear clogs to the market."

He slumped onto his bed. He had a new Scotch-plaid spread. His new curtains featured retrievers, mallards, and men with guns.

"Jesus, Teresa, this is awful. There's AIDS, there's skinheads and rednecks. Dad's just going to shoot me, and Mom is never going to have grandchildren to dress up and take to church."

"Your mom doesn't go to church."

"She'd start."

I settled on the bed right beside him. Larry had his hands in his lap. He looked at them like, Where did these come from? He had on jeans, and a T-shirt so white it almost hurt my eyes. A T-shirt that he'd washed himself. And probably ironed.

I leaned into him.

"What?" he asked. "Are you going to do that stuff now?"

I ran one fingernail down his forearm, made my voice as husky as I could, and said what Mary Ann would say, "Come here, baby."

That sure worked! Larry's face, big as an asteroid, hurtled toward me. His tongue battered at my teeth. "I love you," he moaned. "I do."

"Okay," I said. "That was good. Now I'm supposed to play with your hair, and that'll make you want to grab my boobs."

"I already want to do that."

"Seriously?"

"Absolutely. I always wanted to, but I thought it was rude."

"So should we skip the part where I play with your hair?"

"I think so."

We fell back onto the bed. He grabbed at one breast and twisted like he was trying to open a jar of pickles.

I batted at his hand and sat up.

Panting, he asked, "Did I hurt you?"

"We're just supposed to take our clothes off now."

"Wait." He got off the bed, walked to the window, and looked out at the clouds. "If I was, you know, queer, what would you do?"

"You're not queer."

"But what if I was? What would you do?"

"Nothing."

"It wouldn't matter?"

"Not to me." Actually, I didn't know if it would matter. I didn't think it would. But it sure might to a lot of other people.

"What about Elliot? He's the straightest boy in the world."

"You're not gay, okay?" I played with the top button of my blouse. "Now pay attention. It's time for me to say, *Let's get naked.*"

Mary Ann told me after that, boys would start tearing off their clothes. And hopping around with one shoe off and one shoe on and their pants around their ankles. She said to make sure not to laugh or they'd get really mad.

Instead, Larry reached for a Kleenex and blew his nose. "I'm not taking anything off. I'm fat."

"You're not, either."

He laughed bitterly. "Then why do all my pants have *Husky* on the pocket?"

"We're not supposed to be talking. You're supposed to be staring in awe at my naked body."

"But you're not naked."

"Oh, sorry." I stepped out of my jeans.

Larry just inspected me.

"Those underpants are so white," he said, "there must be a special Eskimo word."

"Lingerie is supposed to drive you crazy," I pointed out. "Do you feel crazy?"

"A little. Maybe. They're just bigger than I thought they'd be."

I looked down. "Bigger how?"

"Just bigger. In the Victoria's Secret catalog, they're never so . . . big. But I'm still awed. Really."

"Good. Mary Ann says now we can either do it, or if I don't want to get pregnant, there are these things I can do to you."

He looked down at the carpet. "I can't do anything right now."

"Why not?"

"It went away."

"What did?"

"You know. *It.*"

"Went away? Where?"

"Pittsburgh. How do I know? It happens all the time. They're fickle."

"You can't get it back?"

He shook his head. "You just get a new one; they're like appliances."

I sat down beside him in my enormous underpants. I took his hand in mine. "So do you want to get a new one?"

"Oh, I don't know. I'm all fucked up."

"Did I do something wrong? Mary Ann says—"

"It's not that."

"Then what? You're not like Elliot, are you? You don't think sex is bad?"

"I think it's confusing. I think it's . . . embarrassing. Shoot, I *know* it's embarrassing. And I think it's, kind of, I don't know—unnecessary."

I was all of a sudden a little cold. I slipped into my jeans, hopping on one foot a little like the poor dumb head-over-heels boy was supposed to do. When I had my pants on again, I asked him, "So what do you think?"

"God, I don't know."

"Do you feel gay?"

He shook his head. "I just feel weird."

"So what? I feel weird most of the time."

That seemed to make him feel better. "You do?"

"You know I do. I call you and say I do."

He reached for me and we sat on the bed again. "Maybe we should just be weird together."

We fell back then and stared at the ceiling. Side by side like that, we probably looked like mummies.

"Do you," he asked finally, "think that Elliot will want to be weird, too?"

LARRY

After breakfast I plod upstairs, shave, and take a shower. This afternoon is Elliot's party. His eighteenth. So I look in my closet, plan what I want to wear.

I turn on the TV to anything (something I would criticize anyone else for). Lo and behold, there's an old black-and-white Tarzan movie with the exquisite Johnny Weissmuller wrestling a fortunate crocodile.

I'll just slip back into bed for a bit.

"Larry. Scooch over."

It's Teresa, looming over me. Puppylike, she sniffs around. "You smell good."

"I just took a shower."

"Were you asleep?"

"Slightly."

She slithers in; one arm goes across my chest, one

leg across both of mine. It's like she's trying to get into a capsized canoe.

"Don't bounce on my stomach; I had venison spaghetti for breakfast." And then there's the effect Johnny Weissmuller has on impressionable youths.

"Venison spaghetti?" She makes a face.

"I know you won't eat that, but I could fix you something else."

"I'm okay."

"Did you eat breakfast?"

"I had an egg."

"One?"

"It was a big egg."

"Did it stay down?"

"So far. You know, I'll bet I'll feel more like eating when we get to California. I like avocados a lot."

"Did you run today?"

"You know I did."

"I should run with you."

"You couldn't keep up. And anyway, you're fine. You lift weights."

"Thank god for Elliot. If he didn't make me work out, I'd ooze through Wendleville devouring everything in sight. What is it with me and my mother, anyway? Every other queer with a cold, distant father does his mother's makeup and picks out her clothes. Every time I lay eyes on mine, I want to eat."

"That's funny. Every time I think of mine, I want to throw up." Now Teresa mounts me completely; she's

like someone riding bareback. "Remember how much
I hated her?"

"Sure."

"And wanted her to die?"

"Childhood is a bloodthirsty period."

"Then she did. Sort of."

"Die?"

"Sort of. Which was what I said I wanted."

"Where is this going, Teresa?"

"So why can't I stop thinking about her?"

There probably isn't an answer to that, and even if
there is, I'm not sure Teresa really wants to hear it. Anyway, I'm thinking about "Childhood is a bloodthirsty
period." I like hearing myself talk because I never
know what I'll say. Or how I'll say it. *Bloodthirsty.*
Where did my facility with words come from? A gift
from the gods, perhaps? Not Elliot's punishing father-
God but another. What else did the gods give me, I
wonder. Good friends, certainly. More than enough
money. Intelligence. And then there's my sexual pref-
erence. What kind of gift is that?

Teresa falls forward, kisses me as innocently as an
aunt. "I also want to kill my father."

If she has an extra ounce of body fat, I can't find it.
Where her shorts bunch up, I can see an inch of white
skin above a solid too-bronze thigh. She is going to be
a wizened old woman.

"Because of Tiny Town?" I ask.

"That is my sole defense, Your Honor. I throw my-self on the mercy of the court."

I kiss her forehead, rake back her dark red hair with my fingers. "It won't be long now, and we are out of here."

"Remember when you were afraid you were queer and I came over? It was five years ago today."

"If this is an anniversary, I didn't get you anything."

"You said my underpants were huge."

"I was nervous."

"You got hot for a minute." She drums on my chest. Keeps drumming as she asks, "Is Kyle coming to El-liot's party?"

"No."

"Good. I hate Kyle."

"Don't be jealous. He's just somebody I see."

"Ah, the euphemisms are beautiful this time of year." She stops pretending I'm a tom-tom. Rubs my chest instead. Vanity makes me tense my pectoral muscles. "Can you sleep some more?" she asks. "I could sleep."

I open my arms. "We'll cuddle. You can take a nap."

She takes my face in her hands. "I love you."

"I love you, too. Now get down here."

A little squirming, a twitch here and there, an im-polite yawn right in my face (I like to look in her mouth, though. She has perfect teeth. Not a filling anywhere.), and she's asleep.

I doze a little and think about five years ago. She meant well. And I did get excited. Just not because of her. *The Last of the Mohicans* was on television. Over her earnest shoulder I watched a bare-chested Daniel Day-Lewis running through the forest in a chamois jockstrap.

4

But the future, I've been there,
and it's not what it used to be.

ELLIOT

When I wake up I'm eighteen. Mom's cooking pot roast (my favorite) for my birthday dinner. My aunts and uncles are coming over. Maybe Larry's mom. Probably not Teresa's father, who never goes anywhere except the Hobby Shop.

I wonder where I'll be a year from now? Will I only get two presents?

Exactly five years ago, Teresa called and said that she was afraid Larry was gay and what did I think. I said I thought she was crazy.

"But," she asked, "are you sure?"

"Sure, I'm sure. He doesn't walk funny, he doesn't talk funny, and he doesn't have a little dog. We're best friends; if anybody'd know, I would."

"Well," she said, "I hope you're right, because this is Wendleville."

"Well," I said, "he's not, so stop talking about it."

I turned out to be wrong about that. I wonder if I'm wrong about going to California?

So today I roll a joint and go down to the pasture to do a little thinking. Guess what? There's a brand-new billboard that reads:

LAKEVIEW ACRES

HOME OF THE FUTURE NOW

Streets, stores, playgrounds, pools—they're all up there in living color. The cars have see-through roofs. Some guy with a briefcase flies to work with a little rocket on his back.

Our Volvo is still down there, but the ground's been leveled and there's all of a sudden a road right down into the pasture where there used to be nothing but switchbacks and bushes and trees and cow pies.

What is it about birthdays, anyway? Last year I had the flu. The one before that somebody ran into my dad's Firebird. Once a refrigerator at the shop went out and a bunch of meat spoiled. Another time I sprained my ankle. Rita left town on my birthday, and then there was Teresa's news about Larry.

Is God trying to tell me something?

TERESA

The thing I really like about Elliot's parties is that I get to see his aunt Anne. She says I can call her anytime. Or drop by her house. I know she means it, but I don't want to get used to that. Anne isn't going to be where Larry, Elliot, and I are going.

I run past her place a lot, though. Accidentally on purpose. She does taxes and financial planning out of her spare room. Their spare room. Hers and Bill's. But I wouldn't want to show up all sweaty while she's trying to get somebody to buy a mutual fund. If she's doing dishes, though, and sees me out the kitchen window, she always waves, comes out with a big glass of water, and fusses over me. I like to be fussed over.

Right after Mom ran away from home, a lot of neighbors brought things to eat, but Anne was the one who really took care of Dad and me. I don't know any other spin to put on that running-away-from-home business. Mom left. Abandoned ship. Do I hate her? Sure. Do I blame her? Not like I used to. I'm about to get the hell out of here, too.

For a while Anne did all the cooking and laundry—just like somebody had died. Which in a way somebody had. She was there when I came in from school, and back by the time I got up in the morning. Doing schoolwork I could hear her from my room upstairs. She sang while she worked. I didn't want her to ever go home.

At night Anne liked to watch *Jeopardy.* She and Larry and I took turns answering the questions. She read my essays before I handed them in and remembered which one went with which class, and asked when I was going to get them back and said if they weren't all A's, she was personally going to have a talk with that teacher. She wanted to know how far I ran and how fast. She made a chart so we could plot my progress. She got my socks almost as white as Larry's.

Then one day she cooked and baked and froze as many casseroles and meat loaves as our freezer would hold. And that night after *Jeopardy,* she stood up and said, "Well, you all are on your own now. I've got a husband who's tired of eating dinner alone."

Then she shook hands with my dad and Larry, hugged me so hard all the breath whooshed out of me,

and got in her little Subaru. Larry and I stood outside
and watched her drive away.

I took a deep breath and swallowed hard. I was not
going to be a wuss. When I got blisters, I popped them
myself. When I tripped over a curb, I got up and bled
while I ran. No way was I going to cry.

Larry put his arm around me. "We're not going to
leave you."

"Who isn't?"

"Elliot and I. We're not going to leave you."

"Elliot might."

He seemed to think that one over. "Maybe, but I
won't." And he pulled me into him.

We were sixteen. He'd been working out for three
years, so he was pretty strong. I shrugged his arm off,
anyway.

"Do what you want," I said. "I don't care."

I'm anxious to see Anne at Elliot's party. I put on some
new blue Nike exercise pants, grab a fleece pullover
but wear only a cropped top that shows off my flat
stomach. I don't want my sad-assed dad there, but I
want to be able to tell the truth when I say, "I asked."

Fourteen basement steps later, there he is—the
Mayor of Nowhere. The console board is in front of
him. Beyond that lies Tiny Town, his miniature king-
dom. All hand-painted. Sometimes with a brush about
as big as an eyelash.

I bet if I picked up my father's free hand, he'd barely have a pulse.

I say, "Probably you don't want to go to this party, either."

"Maybe later."

"Whatever."

He tried to kill himself after Mom left—did I mention that? Went downstairs, took a bunch of pills, and fell asleep on an old sweater of hers. I just happened to walk in and called 911. That's when Anne stepped in. The old suicide watch.

I'm through being patient with him. I know he lost a wife, but I lost a mother! *You can get another wife! Just snap out of it. Take off that stupid engineer's hat. Go to the party. Get drunk. Feel somebody up. Make the most of your life.* That's what Larry and Elliot and I are going to do. We're going to get out of here as soon as we can and make the most of our lives.

LARRY

I'm just getting ready to walk out the door when Elliot calls.

"Guess who showed up?" he says. "Mary Ann."

"So?"

"My mom invited her."

"No way."

"She looks totally different."

"And?"

"And I've got this half-naked girl I invited standing in the kitchen."

"What's Mary Ann doing?"

"Being supernice to everybody."

"Then relax. I'll be there in five minutes."

Mother and I start for the party, walking on the
street's weedy margin. Part of the time she's a little
ahead of me and I see how trim-figured she is in her

J. Jill duds. After being struck by lightning, she rapidly lost forty pounds. Not a diet that will ever make the late-night infomercials.

A truck rumbles by on its way to Lakeview Acres, forcing us toward the culvert. (Every local election, all the candidates promise sidewalks for this end of town, but the sidewalks never materialize.)

"Your father says that development is an eyesore already. He says affordable housing is code for the kind of people who pee off their front porches."

"There goes Dad's membership in the Politically Correct Physicians' Society."

"Your father was never one to mince words."

"My father was never one to *use* words."

Nothing fazes her. I envy her poise.

She says, "We can move if we have to, but other people can't. Teresa's father, for instance. He was counting on his place being worth more, not less."

"When he got hurt, he got a ton of money. Everybody knows that."

My mother nods. "Yes, and he bought some bonds that mature at different times so he has an income. But he's not wealthy by any means."

"Maybe it'll be all right. Maybe whoever moves in will pee indoors."

She shakes her head. "It won't be all right. When you were younger and spent every day down there with your friends, the pasture was a basin of light. Now it's more like a cauldron with a lot of conflicted energy."

"Did the pasture come to you or did you make a house call?"

"It just came up in session."

I stop, and I make her stop. "Don't embarrass me at this party, okay? People treat you like you're some sort of ridiculous fortune-teller."

"No, they don't," she says mildly. "That's how you treat me."

Teresa's back door is always open, and today so is the one to the basement. I meet her as she climbs out of the underworld.

"How's your dad?"

"Screw him. Let's go."

"I'll just say hi."

She smiles at my mother. Reaches for her. "We'll meet you at the party, then."

Any mom in a storm, that's Teresa's motto. Also, she's mad because Milton isn't the father she thinks she wants. Which is an affectionate father. One generally happy to see her. Who wears slides instead of those awful corduroy slippers (*corde du roi:* cloth of the king). Who gets his hair cut regularly, and who had never shouted "All I wanted was a son, and you couldn't even do that" during one of the many noisy showdowns he and Rita had.

Not a lot to ask, actually, when you stop to think about it.

I look at Milton (I cannot bring myself to call him

Milt) from the bottom step. Hard to picture him shout-
ing like a madman. But I believe Teresa, just as I believe the story Rita told Elliot's aunt Stephanie about
how Milton chased her through the house until he
finally brought her down like a wolf that targets the
ailing or confused. It wasn't one of those spirited newly-
wed romps, either, but an honest-to-god pursuit. And
it happened all the time.

"Hi, Mr. Hoagland. It's Larry."

He turns, looks up from the magnifier he'd been
bent over. He has a thin, dictator's mustache but herba-
ceous sideburns. All of it looks glued on. "Why," he
asks, "aren't you at the party?"

"I will be." I point up. "I'm going. How are you
doing?"

He shrugs. I can approach him now that he's seen
me. In a way he's like a preoccupied animal I don't
want to startle.

The lights are on in Tiny Town. The trains, as in
Mussolini's Italy, run on time. I pick up a small magnifying glass. "May I?"

There's a grin on the paperboy working the corner of Elfin and Wee streets; a frown for the teacher,
who is reading poetry, no doubt, since everyone is
sitting in a circle on the lawn of the middle school.
Elliot's father stands outside a diminutive Madison's
Designer Meats, chatting up a woman wearing a
slaughterhouse red dress. The old Toon's is there, too,
with its rack of newspapers by the door.

That's remarkable enough. But in a bungalow's bedroom, I find a man asleep in his shirt, socks, and underpants while a woman with long red hair sits at a desk.

I lean closer. "Is there ink in that inkwell?"

"Just a microgram."

He is such an odd man. Magnifying glass in hand, I step past him and move, like the sun, west. At the local plunge lies a sunbather with hair under her arms. Someone carries a stricken collie with blood on its muzzle toward the animal hospital. At the edge of the forest, there's a hunter in the grip of an enormous grizzly. And he's already installed a decrepit SNAKEVIEW ACRES—half-collapsed houses, a fetid backwater, tiny serpents everywhere. Voodoo is his way of dealing with progress.

"This gets more amazing all the time."

He nods, eyes down like a Chinese bride's. Then waits for me to at least acknowledge Boys' Town, an entire block dedicated to what he thinks is a gay life-style: half-naked men on a loading dock, shirtless men with poodles out for a stroll, bare-chested men at an outdoor café.

He started Boys' Town a few years ago. He meant well, I suppose. It's hard to be sure. If it's authenticity he values, why doesn't he have skinheads with baseball bats prowling the backstreets, and fervid Christians with GOD HATES FAGS placards? By now everybody in Wendleville knows I'm gay. And the perceptive might have known before I did. Every year it gets a little harder to live here.

Now I'm angry, but I shake it off as I walk to the party. I wave to Mrs. Edleman, whose bungalow is like something out of a coloring book—green lawn, red brick, gray roof, blue bird, brown tree. Then there's Mr. Walski's place, where everything tilts—house, garage, doghouse, shed. Is it because Mr. Walski came back from Desert Storm limping instead of walking? Can animate matter influence inanimate? That's the kind of thing Teresa and I can talk about for hours.

I hear the party before I see it. A pickup game is in progress on the immaculate driveway that Luke, Elliot's father, had poured so his son could practice.

By the way, isn't Luke the perfect name for him? No one ever thinks of the Bible, I'll bet, or Saint Paul, who called Luke a "most dear physician." It's a gunslinger's name or a French-cinema thug smoking a Gauloise.

Today Luke is in white warm-up pants, white T-shirt, white Converse high-tops. He is some dazzling apparition. The local dreamboat. A stand-in for someone almost pretty, like Tom Cruise or a matured Justin Timberlake. Luke is a former marine decorated for valor. So other men forgive him his beauty. Years ago I once heard a man in Toon's say, "Ah, it's not his fault." As if being handsome were a liability. Something to be overlooked. And pardoned.

"Larry!" He jogs my way, holds up one hand so I

know to return not a regular how's-the-missus shake but a much hipper NBA semi–soul brother grip. "How's it hangin'?"

"I'm not sure, Luke. But I could check."

"You crack me up, kid." His arm goes around my shoulders. "C'mon, let's shoot some hoops."

Five years ago today, this driveway was still gravel and grass. Five years ago today, Elliot met me on the back steps and dragged me toward the hollyhocks at the southwest corner of the garage. "You are not queer, do you hear me?"

"Okay."

"I mean it, Larry."

"I said okay."

"Okay what? Say it."

"Okay, I'm not queer."

He punched me in the arm. Hard. "Well, don't forget it."

"Whatever you say."

"Not 'Whatever you say.' Hit me back."

"I don't want to hit you back. I don't want to hit anybody."

He stalked away, turned on his heel, shouted, "I'm already teaching you how to lift weights! Do I have to teach you how to fight, too?"

But Elliot's not exasperated today. He's just waiting for the game to start again. He tosses the ball off to my right because he wants me to catch it with one hand gracefully, then shoot one from downtown.

Why not. We practiced this move often enough.
Swish.

Elliot's uncles, Bill and Chris, applaud. "We'll take him. We need three-on-two. Get your ass over here, Larry. They're killing us."

I've known these men all my life, but we shake hands anyway: First there's Bill, who owns a small fleet of trucks and always wears Frye boots and jeans. Then Chris, who recently opened another two bakeries in Springfield. He leases a huge Mercury Mountaineer in case, I suppose, he has to drive over an Alp-sized cream puff. He's in hard-soled Florsheims, slacks, and a sport shirt with hula girls on it.

Elliot's a jock, handsome and popular. He could have a huge party, but he wants things like they've always been—his parents, his aunts and uncles, Teresa and me.

Chris asks, "How are you, my man?"

"Oh, you know—struggling to survive demonic forces in an apocalyptic setting. Otherwise, not bad."

"I meant, smart-ass, are you getting any?"

This is a game we play, a game within a game: He'll be one of the guys; I'll pretend to be.

"Make him," says Bill, "say something in Spanish."

Chris gets me in a harmless headlock. It's all horseplay. I'm half disgusted, half flattered. These guys know I'm queer, but at least I'm different from the ones on TV, for instance, with their exquisite taste in clothes and towels. I'm queer but not *that* queer. Odd, maybe.

Queer in that sense. And devoted to Teresa. Absolutely.
As well as to Elliot. But no, not in that way. Oh no. Elliot's all boy.

I take hold of the waistband of Chris's Dockers like
Elliot taught me, get my knee behind one of his, and
down on the lawn we go. He hits hard but holds on.
Chris deserves some credit: Not every man in town
would even touch me, much less wrestle. A few call me
names from the cabs of their inevitable, it seems, pick-
ups. Others, circumspect and suspicious, treat me like
some shy herbivore.

He's not holding me tight. "You better speak Spanish, you son of a bitch, before Bill comes over here and
sits on you."

*"El hombre en el rincón lleva los pantalones muy apre-
tados."*

Bill scratches his head. "How do you do that? Guys
on the job jabber in Mex all day long. You'd think it'd
sink in."

"If I was as smart as you," Chris says brushing at his
pants, "I'd have bakeries on Mars."

We watch a skip loader rumble by on its way to the
pasture. Luke says, "The mayor came in the shop the
other day and acted like he didn't have anything to do
with the permits for Lakeview. Who builds cheap
houses down in a pasture, anyway? When it rains
they're going to float away."

"What'd he get under the table?" asks Bill. "That's
what I'd like to know."

Chris suggests, "You can't hold on to the past, boys. Progress is good."

Elliot has had enough. "Ball up, guys. C'mon. Fawn's watching. Make me look good."

Who's Fawn?

My teammates try to contain Elliot, but he's a phantom. If Chris rushes, he eludes him first, then Bill. If they both charge, he seems to walk right through them as if they were mist.

That leaves me against Luke. Besides teaching me how to shoot a creditable free throw, Elliot also made me learn to read my opponent. For example, Luke loses his temper easily, and then his poise and concentration.

Two times in a row the big showboat taunts me with the ball; both times I knock it out of his hands and out of bounds. Once rattled, he can't hit anything; then he loses his temper. So when we both go for a rebound, he gives me an elbow to the jaw. I shove and down he goes, tearing his pants.

"You son of a bitch," he says. "These were brand-new."

I hold out one hand, as I've been taught in Sportsmanship School. He takes it and I pull him to his feet.

He's glad that I'm not some smirking ponce, but he's still disgusted from being tripped up by the local homo. He points to my cheek. "You're bleeding."

I glance at his knee. "You, too."

"Maybe we need a nurse."

"Maybe you do, you candy-ass." I'm just reading off the trash talk crib sheet Elliot made for me.

Luke's in my face again, still smelling like Old Spice aftershave. It rises off him like steam. I remember the ads—a sailor with a duffel over one shoulder, a pretty girl at the window waiting.

Suddenly—"What a bunch of faggots."

Now Luke turns toward the street. I know without looking that it's Billy and his faithful companion, Witless Drew. It's Billy slumped in the driver's seat, half a sneer on his stupid face. It's Billy who's taunting us.

I just snap and charge the truck. Of course when I get there, I don't know what to do. I don't want to strangle him. And I've never hit anybody in my life.

So I grab his nose.

Both of Billy's hands come off the wheel. He follows his nose—he has to—until his head and one shoulder are out the window.

I hear myself say, "I'd apologize if I were you."

Luke is right beside me. Elliot and Bill and Chris gather around.

Luke orders, "Twist it a little harder, Larry. I don't think he heard you."

I pretend to but don't.

"I 'ory," Billy moans.

"Pardon me?" I put one hand to my ear.

"I'm thorry."

"For . . . ?"

"For saying you were faggots."

"For saying *they* were faggots. I *am* a faggot."

Billy's face is vermilion. I wish I didn't like this so much.

Then I let go. Billy's hands spring to his face and massage his glowing snout.

"You homo bastard," he snarls at me. "You're dead meat." He reaches for the shift on the old truck, pops the clutch, throws gravel.

Luke grins at me. "Way to go, tiger."

I take a deep breath. "I'm sick of guys like him." I can't stop shaking. Am I just relieved that I didn't act like some timorous fairy? Or am I thrilled by the idea of mayhem? And if so, is there a place for me on some WWF SmackDown! as the Ferocious Fruit?

Chris drifts up beside me. "Listen, man, those guys aren't kidding."

His hand is on my shoulder, and I shrug it away. "Screw them."

"His dad was trouble, and he's trouble. You watch your step."

I'm swept toward the house right about then. The others are whooping and patting each other on the back. Chris tousles my carefully moussed hair; Bill shoves me playfully. Jostling each other like Thoroughbreds going around the first turn, we burst through the back door into the kitchen. Everyone's there; they've been watching—like the Old Spice girl—through the window.

Crowd noise: "What happened?" "What was all that about?" "Oh, you're hurt." "You're bleeding!"

Teresa has a bemused glance for me. I shrug and let Mary Ann lead me to a kitchen chair. She is as brisk and efficient as the nurse she wants to be and now actually resembles. Luke is right beside me, his pants leg rolled above a well-toned calf.

Everyone wants to know who that was in the driveway.

"Some boy from school."

Then they want to know what his problem is.

"Just a misunderstanding."

"Are you all right?"

"I'm perfectly all right." And it's true. I'm glad I did it. I wish I'd ripped Billy's beating heart from his chest and devoured it. Well, maybe not that.

Elliot's aunt Anne, armed with Bactine and cotton, ministers to me. His mom handles Luke, kneeling between his spraddled legs, shaking her head, which means, "Tssk-tssk-tssk, men." But she has her free hand draped across one solid thigh. She glances up at him and he won't take his eyes off her. If they were alone, she'd be on her back on this spotless floor, making a joyful noise. When she lectures her son, it isn't sex she disapproves of. It's sex out of—she actually uses this word on him—*wedlock*.

When Luke and I have been kissed and made better, everybody gets something to drink. Something non-alcoholic, at least in the kitchen with its butcher-block island, its copper-bottomed pans, its picture of Jesus knocking on the door of the United Nations Building.

The living room is in another, more liberal county. Bill always has a silver flask. They pass it around, surreptitiously pour from it, and rehash my triumph. Teresa excuses herself and heads for the guest bathroom. Elliot leads a girl who must be Fawn toward the den. I decide to go back to the kitchen, where the ladies start whispering about something called perimenopause. How complicated their bodies are. While mine or Elliot's seems simple as a Swiss toy.

Elliot's aunt Stephanie checks to make sure we are mostly alone. I'm not one of the girls, but I'm not one of those in the living room, either. I'm something else.

"I can imagine leaving a husband," says Stephanie, "especially one like Milt. But who could turn her back on her own child?"

Three heads shake in unison. On cue Anne brushes at her cheek with the back of one hand. "Look at what it did to that family. Milt is a wreck and Teresa can't weigh ninety pounds."

"She doesn't eat," says Stephanie. "I never see her eat. She just pushes the food around on her plate."

Anne says, "When Rita left and I stayed over there for a while, she ate my cooking."

"We'll make sure she eats today."

"Don't," Anne warns, "make a big deal out of it."

"Does she throw up like those skinny girls on television?" Stephanie asks.

Anne shakes her head. "No. She's just high-strung."

"And when it comes to that obsessive running," says Elliot's mother, "you don't have to be a psychologist to know she's running away from something."

That's a new one. I've heard this conversation a dozen times, and only bother to listen for the variations, like an anthropologist tracking a popular folktale by firelight.

They don't even know the whole story. Only what Milton told Anne. But I know more. On the day she left, Teresa's mom packed one bag, said a few ugly things, and made her exit. Then a few seconds later reappeared. "You're making me up, anyway!" she shouted. "To meet your own needs. Whoever the hell I am, I am not that person."

One of the reasons I love Teresa is her honesty. After she told me everything her mother said, she confessed, "It's true, isn't it? I did make her up."

Such insight, however, does not always keep her from calling me at night and crying, or from clinging to Anne at every opportunity. Not that either of us minds.

When Elliot's mother goes into the dining room for a platter, Anne—a stout little page with her buttoned-up collars, calf-length skirts, sturdy boots, and useless womb—sidles right up to her sister. "I saw Luke and a blonde the other day."

"Where?" Stephanie demands, louder than necessary.

"At the shop."

"Well, I saw him at the shop with a blonde, a brunette, and a redhead. God, Anne—it's where he works. People come in to buy things."

"This one wasn't just interested in his pork loin."

"It's not his fault. He's so good-looking, women throw themselves at him." Stephanie tugs at my mother. "Tell her, Esther. Tell her what you told me."

Mother glances at me; I look away. "I just said that Luke is a very young soul, and in this lifetime he's interested in flesh; that's all. I mean, look at the profession he chose. It doesn't mean he's unfaithful."

"So there!" Stephanie actually puts both fists on her hips and looks very Falstaffian. Then she catches my eye. I nod and hold up two fingers, one for each minute. Then I rise and prepare myself for our assignation.

The garage where Luke, Elliot, and I work out is spotless. With an expensive piece of carpet discreetly taped at the edges so it won't unravel. And equipped with a Universal machine (bench press, lat pull-down, dip bar), stair-climber, and shiny dumbbells. An old black weight rack reminds us all what pumping iron used to be like before sissified padded benches and chrome everything.

Stephanie, who slipped out the front door claiming, "The air is fresher outside," is nervous and picks up a five-pound weight. Curls it awkwardly, even for a woman who has never worked a day in her life, has a girl come in to clean and make lunch, and who goes out to dinner with her husband six nights a week.

I know how to wait. I lean against a wall hung with testosterone pinups: Luke with an enormous fish; Luke with a bowling ball; Luke and my father with a hundred slain doves at their feet.

Stephanie tells me, "I shouldn't be getting this stuff from you. It gives you the upper hand. You don't have some client list the cops could find, do you?"

"Stephanie, you called me. This is a favor. It costs three hundred dollars, but it's still a favor. Kyle's not making a cent and neither am I."

"I smoke too much, but if I don't I get anxious." She hands me the cash; I hand over the Baggie.

Out come her rolling papers. Suddenly she's all business, all focus and concentration. As sure-handed as a surgeon.

Then my little gold lighter. A long drag. The invitation.

I lean forward. "Sure."

"God, I just had to get out of that house. In the kitchen it's Victoria and her old-time religion; in the living room it's either how tough you are all of a sudden or that bullshit about how Elliot won the big game. Elliot didn't win the big game. He passed the ball to Bobby Reed, and Bobby Reed won the big game."

"It's revisionist history," I say. "If you say something happened often enough, pretty soon everybody else says so, too."

"Is he going to graduate?"

"Elliot? Of course he's going to graduate."

"Thanks to you and Teresa."

"It's not like we took the tests for him."

"You just wait. You think you're so smart now, you and Terri—"

"*Teresa*. She hates to be called Terri."

"You and Terri and Elliot. You'll see. Things don't work out like you plan. Take it from me."

I return the joint. "Are you sure marijuana is the drug for you, Stephanie? Most people just giggle and eat Oreos, but you get a little—"

"You're lucky you've got school to go to." She's still got a lungful, so her voice is high and tight. "But what do you do after that?"

The dope is smooth. The room gets very distinct and crisp edged. The weights glisten invitingly. "Read, listen to language tapes, talk on the phone."

She points toward the house. "To those two?"

"We're friends."

"We, we, we. Don't you ever do anything on your own?"

"Why should I?"

"I read that essay you wrote, the one that won the prize, the one they printed in the *State Journal-Register.*"

"And?"

"Did you have to use all the big words you know in one sentence?"

I have a large vocabulary, but it's not only that. I think slang is ugly and certain grammatical constructions hurt my ears. So? I am who I am. Or as Kyle says, "There are all kinds of sissies. You're that kind."

Stephanie inhales deeply. "I barely recognized Mary Ann. What's with the new look?"

I shrug. "She did Bad Girl for a long time. Now she must be doing Nice Girl."

"Is Elliot into that?"

"Who knows."

"Well, are they still together?"

"Not lately."

"You know what I don't understand? I don't understand why Luke married Victoria. She's such a drag."

She is really a loose cannon today; it's just one topic after another. Then (thank god) Elliot knocks on the window, his eyebrows up interrogatively. I motion him and the new girl in.

Stephanie waves her hands around wildly. "Are you crazy?"

"It's not like he doesn't know. We do this every time we get together."

She takes another hit. Says in her munchkin voice, "Really?"

I'm finally introduced to Fawn in her low-slung jeans and Britney Spears lip gloss. I make fun of my mother, the local Sibyl, but I can see into the future, too. Fawn's a pretty little thing under the tarty garnish. In a few years she'll marry someone who's figuratively, if not literally, portly and take pleasure in teaching her daughters to swim at the country club.

Elliot, though, is nervous. He's usually very hands-on about his conquests, but not this one. It could be because of the general disapproval in the kitchen, or perhaps it's the new salubrious Mary Ann, right now probably looking through his mother's cookbooks and asking which recipes are Elliot's favorites.

5

. . . succinct and definitive days, finished.

ELLIOT

I know it's crummy with Fawn around, but I kind of hoped the new Mary Ann was watching from the kitchen. Okay, so it wasn't the NBA or summer league or even high school level. It was just driveway ball, uncle ball, birthday ball.

I still looked good. I was still in the zone. Man, I was guarding Uncle Bill once, took the ball right out of his hands, hooked it without even looking, and I got nothing but net. (My back is to the basket, right? Picture that!)

By Zoots, I'll miss this. I will. I'll miss it bad. Larry says there'll be a YMCA wherever we go, though, and he's right. I'd like to play at the beach in LA, too, like Woody Harrelson in *White Men Can't Jump,* if Larry would promise not to hit on the local Wesley Snipes while I'm around.

Speaking of hitting on people, that's how I met Fawn. She and some of her friends drove over from Springfield one day last week just to check Wendleville out. I happen to pull up next to them at a stop sign. Before you know it, we're at Burger King. The funny thing is, I didn't particularly want to hook up. I mean, I did it sort of on automatic. Like a guy who's full but keeps eating just because there's still food on the table.

Eventually they get back into Fawn's car (her mom's, actually, because it's a Saturn wagon, and nobody in her right mind would ever pick that if she had a choice) and drive off.

Leaving me staring at her phone number and feeling really—to use a Larry word—*forlorn.*

That's sad-sounding, isn't it? You'd never name a dog that or a sports franchise. (The Jerseyville Panthers beat the Fayetteville Forlorns 101-6 last night. Ha-ha.)

Okay, now I'm serious again. Because I was serious when I called Teresa for advice. I mean, there I was with a new girl lined up, but I just felt tired. I asked Teresa what was wrong with me, and she said maybe I was a victim of repetition and anonymity. Or in terms even I can understand—same old same old.

Then I asked her if girls ever felt that way.

Teresa said they do: Introduce the new guy to your parents, laugh at the new guy's dumb jokes, push the new guy's dumb hands away. But what does she know? She never goes out with anybody but Larry and me, and those aren't dates. I'd ask Larry, but he's . . . well,

Larry. Or maybe I should ask him anyway. Because Larry and Teresa know me deep down. Better than I know myself, probably.

I've told them stuff I've never told anybody, like how every time I get sick, I think it's because I've been bad and God is punishing me. Larry says *good* and *bad* are relative terms. Teresa reminds me how my mom acted when I brought this girl Amber home for dinner, and because she smoked, Mom wouldn't even talk to her. How good was that? Larry says to forget about good and bad and simply try to be kind. And not just to other people but to myself, too. Especially to myself.

Which is good advice but also kind of weird. Teresa says Larry calls himself names because he hates himself. I guess I hate myself sometimes, and Teresa says she hates herself all the time.

D—, I guess, huh? For the massive digressions. Sorry. The fact is, Fawn (Remember her?) watched me play. She caught my no-look hoop and my many thefts off my uncles, not to mention that scene with Billy. I wish Larry had totally cleaned that guy's clock. Where did he learn that lame nose-move? Tell me it's not some gay thing. Tell me there's no gay martial arts.

Then Larry had a little tiny cut on his face from some under-the-boards scuffle, so he got fussed over, which he likes and which his mother never does for him, being she's in outer space most of the time.

Now, I want to get Fawn out of the kitchen because my mom is acting like she (Fawn) doesn't exist. Mom is all appalled about Fawn's pants, but she's cozy with Mary Ann, who she invited over without asking me because Mom said that she likes what Mary Ann is doing with her life now that she's in the nursing program and has taken that metal in her face to the recycling center and her hair's all natural. Mary Ann's also nice to Fawn. Not phony nice, either. They talk about bands a little (they both like the Dixie Chicks); then she helps her arrange some olives because Fawn is, like, all thumbs.

Out the back door, I see Larry mosey (he thinks nobody knows what's up, but he doesn't mosey unless something is) into the garage, and when Fawn and I get out there, he and Stephanie are toking up. Stephanie acts all oh-my-god-I-can't-smoke-with-my-nephew, but then we finish that doobie plus another one. Stephanie is cool with Fawn, asking her about school and where did she get those jeans and stuff like that. And my aunt is a total craftsman when it comes to rolling a joint.

Then Larry and I see who can bench the most, and I win even though he outweighs me. (And okay, maybe he let me win, because: 1. He's a good guy. And/or 2. Who's he need to impress?)

Anyway, Stephanie and Fawn want to try lifting then (we're pretty buzzed). So I set the weight rack at, like, minus two. They're unbelievably lame, laughing so hard they fall off the bench. We have a good time, but that doesn't stop me from thinking about Mary Ann.

TERESA

I come out of the guest bathroom, with its little bars of soap, its perfect hand towels, and its look-who-still-loves-Martha Stewart collection of lotions and shampoos. I take a couple over-the-shoulder pictures (Who knows what bathrooms are up to when nobody's looking?), then bump into Elliot.

"When was the last time," I ask him, "anybody spent the night?"

"Here? Like, never."

"So who's all the stuff in the bathroom for, the Unseen Guest?" I mean the poem that hangs in his mother's kitchen:

> *Christ is the Head of this house;*
> *the Unseen Guest*
> *at every meal;*
> *the Silent Listener*
> *to every conversation.*

Elliot grimaces. "Don't kid around. Mom might hear."

"I was just thinking that if the guest is unseen, maybe the miniature shaving gel should be unseen, too. You know, tit for tat: Unseen Guest, unseen gel for His unseen beard."

"And don't say T-I-T, either."

I walk him toward the living room, past the big sofa packed with men, and stop in the dining room. Then I point to the kitchen, where his mother and her sisters are getting dinner ready. *His* dinner. The birthday boy. And the birthday boy's very visible date.

"I wish," he says, "she wasn't showing so much skin."

I look at Fawn in her $POILED ROTTEN cropped top. I have better abs; besides running, I do sit-ups every day. But she has better everything else. Is that why he prefers her to me, the shallow bastard?

"So," he asks, "whaddya think?"

I've got my camera to one eye, and I'm waiting for Fawn to bound through the frame. "What do I think about what?"

"Fawn, what else?"

I watch her with the other women. The new Mary Ann arranges pickles and olives on the relish tray, but none of the others (not Elliot's aunts, not his mom, not Larry's mom) can keep their eyes off that tattoo on the small of Fawn's back; it's a Greek cross, not a Christian one, but I bet they don't know that. I zoom in and take three quick pictures: One tells me that Stephanie wants some body art of her own; Anne's frown says that Fawn's tattoo will get in the way of her first MRI; and Victoria shakes her head so hard that the image blurs.

He says, "I didn't think she'd dress like that. I told her on the phone it was my birthday; she knew my mom'd be here, for Zoots' sake."

I give up. "'Zoots'?"

"That old god. The Greek one. Who's dead."

"It's Zeus. But why—"

"Since he's dead, I figure Zoots doesn't care if I take his name in vain."

"Elliot, you dumbshit." I put one hand on his arm. "It's *Zeus.* Rhymes with *juice.*"

"Are you sure?"

"We could ask Larry."

Elliot points. "I keep thinking about that thing that happened in the driveway."

"Why?"

"I just wish they'd had a fair fight and got it over with. Larry made Billy look bad, you know? He isn't going to forget that."

"Billy can't remember his own phone number."

"Maybe. I just hope Larry never meets those guys in a dark alley."

We drift toward the hall that leads to his parents' bedroom, the scene of sanctioned marital sex. From there we can't see Fawn appalling his mother. We can see Larry pretend to watch a game between Somebody U and Somebody Tech. I can sense Elliot admiring

Mary Ann, with her dog-biscuit brown hair and practical shoes. How did that happen so fast? And why? I know her, so I hate her less than I hate Fawn. But I hate everyone he likes. *Talk to* me, *stupid!*

"Aren't you," he asks plaintively, "going to miss all this?"

That's better. "We'll make new friends. People our age."

"But we can't come home again. Ever."

If Larry were here, we'd do some Thomas Wolfe jokes, but they'd be lost on Elliot.

"Don't worry. You'll be the prodigal son and your parents will forgive you."

He gets that innocent look I can't resist. "Promise?"

I snap a picture before he can pose and ruin everything.

"What's it going to be like?" he asks. "When we get where we're going?"

He sounds like we're going to California in a covered wagon.

Larry drifts by just then, shaking an empty Coke can. "What are we talking about?"

"We were," I tell him, "talking about Fawn. Now we're talking about running away from home."

"Speaking of Fawn. What's her last name? The boys in the living room were asking."

Elliot reaches for the empty can. "Let me get you another one of those."

Larry and I exchange a look. Something's up.

"Out with it, Elliot."

"I'm not telling you guys. You'll make fun of her."

Larry and I nod together. We say, "So?"

Elliot sighs. "It's Lively. Fawn Lively. And shut up."

"Gee," Larry muses, "when she fills out one of those applications that say *Last Name First,* it reads Lively Fawn."

My turn. "Seems like she could score some Native American scholarship money with a name like that."

"See? That's why I didn't want to tell you!"

I put one arm around Elliot's waist; Larry does, too. "Forget Fawn," he says. "What are the chances of you two getting married and having a little tattooed tot for Grandma to take to the exorcist?"

"When we get to California," I croon, "we'll have a huge apartment."

"Where?" he asks, like I'm telling him a bedtime story.

"Downtown," Larry says, "in the center of everything. We'll have a car, but we won't use it except on weekends. Everything we need will be within walking distance: movies, plays, museums, fine yet inexpensive restaurants, and let's not forget wonderfully sordid side streets that soon turn into charming paths that lead to a forest where even the wolves are in love with you."

He tightens his grip on me. On us. This is what I like. Now I'm happy.

Then we wander into the kitchen together where

Mary Ann is paging through a cookbook. Larry gets a fresh Coke; Elliot leads Fawn to a corner to thaw her out because his mother's disapproval has given the poor thing goose bumps. I wish he'd throw a blanket over her.

I finally get to talk to Anne. Who puts both arms around me. Who gives me an ear-ringing kiss. (I think of those messages on valentine candies: *A Big Smack-eroo for You!*) I want her to kiss me again. Not like we're gay or anything. I just want her to kiss me.

"How are you, honey?" Even her voice is warm. She smells like vanilla.

She doesn't let go of me and I don't let go of her. We stand there, whispering to each other.

"Are your grades good?" Anne murmurs.

"They're perfect."

"Did you send out those applications we talked about?"

"Yes." She's interested in me. She cares what happens to me.

"Have you heard back?"

I nod, glad we're whispering. Nobody knows about this. Not even Larry or Elliot. Especially not Larry or Elliot. "I got in everywhere: U of I, Purdue, Pitzer. Everywhere."

"Full scholarships?"

"Almost all."

"That's my girl."

I'm shameless. I hold on to her. I want her to say it again.

Larry asks, "Would you two like to be alone?"

Anne shoves him away playfully. "Shush, you. You're just jealous."

He sips his cola. "You see right through me to my baser nature."

"If it's a little sugar you want, just say so. I've got it to spare." She steps back, then opens her arms wide, wider than she did for me. Larry bends a little at the knees and picks her up. Anne squeals, "God, you're strong! And solid as a rock."

I raise my camera, play the good sport. But I wish it were a gun. I want to kill them both. Or maybe just him. Then make Anne tell me I'm her girl. Or make her write on the board a hundred times: *I will not encourage others.* Or have her write on me: *I will love only you.*

I am truly pathetic.

Thank god there's stuff to do: potatoes to mash, lemon peel to grate, and silver to polish. I particularly like to add orange sections to orange Jell-O, because they look like the bodies of lost hikers in some huge, tasty glacier.

Larry settles into a chair and frowns at the olives that Fawn arranged. They look like tiny barrels that rolled off a truck after a wreck in Tiny Town. I'm so glad my father's not here, that full-time killjoy.

Mary Ann takes fresh chips and dip into the living

room. Elliot leads Fawn outdoors, maybe so she can graze? When he's gone, his mother says, "He's so worldly. What could have possessed him to date a girl who dresses like that?"

Anne steps forward. "Don't blame him. Why didn't her parents say something?"

Elliot's mother sighs. "If he would just listen to his inner voice."

"He will," Anne says. "He's young."

"I had so hoped that he'd respond to a higher calling."

Stephanie, Anne, and I look at one another. *Whose turn is it?* Because this is a tough one. Even Larry's mom is mum. I guess she left her crystal ball at home.

"Let's not forget Saul," Larry says finally, "on the road to Damascus."

God bless him; it's the perfect answer: If Saul could turn into Paul, there's hope for Elliot.

Elliot's mother dries her hands, signals Larry to rise (very tsarina-like, if you ask me), and embraces him.

I don't bother to raise the camera; I just shoot from the hip. Stephanie pretends to need "a breath of fresh air." Larry sneaks out the other way.

When we're alone, Elliot's mother sighs. "I pray for Larry every day. We don't hate the sinner, we hate the *sin.*"

LARRY

After the party Elliot walks Teresa and me out toward
the driveway, past Luke's ridiculous Firebird parked
kitty-cornered on the lawn, past the basketball court.

"I gotta get back," he says. "Fawn is watching TV
with Chris, but I don't want to leave her alone too long."

"Where," I ask, "did she come from?"

"Just . . . don't even. I made a mistake, okay?"

Teresa yawns. Once Elliot says good-bye, we'll be on
our way home. My mother left an hour ago; Teresa's
father, as expected, never showed up.

"Man," Elliot says, "I got a lot of presents."

We just nod.

"Do you guys ever feel funny when you get a lot
of stuff for your birthday or Christmas?"

I tell him that I wouldn't know. "I just get chunks
of coal."

Teresa says, "I got an orange once."

Elliot scowls. "I'm not kidding. It's kind of like when I go out with some girl and she's got on a new sweater or something that I know she bought just for me, and I want to tell her, 'I'm not worth it.' Do you ever feel that way?"

"You mean as I sit pawing over my collection of bituminous rocks?"

He absolutely erupts. "Will you fucking take me serious for a change!"

Teresa steps out from under my arm and says, "God heard that, birthday boy. You're in trouble now. No way you're not going to hell, and when you get there all you're going to do is shoot free throws that never go in."

Elliot shakes an accusatory finger. "You're no better than him, Teresa."

Grammatically, it should be no better than *he,* but I don't think this is a good time to point that out. Instead I apologize. He pretends to study the toes of his good shoes. So I add, "And the answer is yes, Elliot. Everybody feels unworthy about ninety percent of the time. But you don't have to tonight. You got all that stuff because those people love you and want the best for you."

"You're not just saying that?"

I shake my head.

"Well, that U of I gear from my dad made me feel really crappy."

Teresa's delivery is very mild, very consoling. "Wear

it in California," she says. "Other people with vowels on their clothes will want to talk to you."

"Yeah, well, maybe I'll meet somebody nicer than you two." But he doesn't mean it. He even adds, "Sorry I yelled at you. And I'm sorry I used the F-word, okay?"

He wants to kiss and make up, so Teresa lets him. I get the handshake.

Then he adds, "I gotta say I kind of missed opening presents from you guys."

Teresa is incredulous. "You said to save our money for California. You said to not get you anything this time."

"I guess I meant anything *big*."

Once we're out of earshot, Teresa starts to laugh. "I can't believe it. Is half the money we saved going to go for presents?"

"Maybe he'll bring his mother's credit card!"

"By the way, his mother is praying for you."

"All my troubles are over."

"See, she doesn't hate the *sinner*, she hates the *sin*."

"And what sin would that be—intolerance? I swear to god, I don't know what's worse: Victoria praying for me or Billy out to get me."

Teresa takes my hand and we walk like Jack and Jill. It's not late, but we're the only ones on the street. The people inside the little houses are asleep or watching TV.

"My father," Teresa says, "is in Lilliput. Want to come in?"

I tell her I can't. "I promised Kyle I'd call."

6

*What is the body, anyway, but a
drawer of old valentines?*

ELLIOT

Fawn tries to help Mom clean up, but it's like washing dishes with Frosty the Snowman. I get her to her car, put a couple of halfhearted moves on her so she can tell her girlfriends she's irresistible, then say good-bye. I'll never see her again. I don't even want to see her again. I don't know what I want, unless it's to be ten years old and down in the pasture with everything like it used to be.

Except then I couldn't walk Mary Ann home. On the way, I start to think about bouncing from LA to Frisco to god-knows-where. Why? Just so I can be with two people who think they're smarter than me?

Mom's right. I have to grow up sometime. Just because some people treat me like a kid doesn't mean I am one.

TERESA

"I promised Kyle I'd call"? How could he say something like that? *"I promised Kyle I'd call"*? Jesus, Joseph, and Mary, why am I even thinking about going anywhere with him and Elliot? My god, I'm as loony as my father. Is there anything tinier than a town with three citizens?

LARRY

When I call Kyle, he talks me into driving to Springfield to meet him. I couldn't be more than two blocks from home when I see Billy's truck in my rearview mirror.

7

*This is the day not
dissected by minutes.*

ELLIOT

When I hear what happened, I track down Billy and beat the shit out of him.

TERESA

When I hear, I open the kitchen drawer with the knives:
Pick me, they cry. Instead I stagger to the door that leads
to Tiny Town and look down. How many movies have
Larry and I seen with someone crumpled at the foot of
a staircase? I lean a little, both hands on the doorjambs
like a skydiver. Then take off running because I want
what running gives me: a way out.

It doesn't happen. Larry is everywhere: standing
outside the Teen Canteen with the smokers, mostly
tough kids who'd take a light from his little gold Ron-
son but would never let their straight hands touch his
queer one.

I see him coming out of Toon's with a magazine
and a Butterfinger; going into the library, the door closing behind him; pushing a grocery cart back to Kroger's
because he could never just leave one in the parking lot.

He's watching Elliot shoot hoops at the high school, wearing his baseball cap backward because Elliot told him he had to; he's coming out of the bank, he's going into church, he's driving his black 4Runner.

I want to go somewhere, anywhere he's never been, where *we've* never been. But where is that? Not in town, that's for sure. But not out of town, either. I know all the back roads because Larry and Elliot taught me to drive on them. We even wanted to buy that summerhouse on Bethel Road someday: ten acres with a pond, green John Deere tractor, red barn, and some e. e. cummings white chickens.

Larry said friends would call for directions from the airport outside Springfield. And he and I and Elliot would sit on the porch, drink lemonade, and wait for them, looking out over the lawn with its volunteer hollyhocks. If it got too warm up there, we'd move toward the big oak and sit in what Larry called the "shady shade."

I think the Bethel house will make me cry. I think when I see it I'll just burst into tears and that'll be that.

But it doesn't. The house only makes it worse, drives everything I'm feeling in deeper. So I just run faster. Run more. Stop to throw up. And run again. I find myself off the road, off the beaten path. (And without him, isn't that where I am, anyway?) I run through acres of corn with its knifelike blades and bludgeony stalks.

I run until it's dark. I run until I can't run anymore.

Then I limp toward home, but only toward. I don't want to see my ridiculous father. He's probably too busy, anyway, adding a mite-sized murder site to the outskirts of Tiny Town.

I go into the pasture, down into it. I follow the new road past the one model home, with its bare bulb dangling from a bare cord in the bare living room and one fat guard asleep in a beat-up Barcalounger on the dumb little porch.

Somebody has moved our Volvo. Now it's crouched on its axles in the underbrush. It still smells like us, though: cheap perfume from Elliot's girlfriends, cigarette smoke mingled with weed, Larry's Oreos stashed under the seat.

I can't believe my dumb body sees those cookies and wants to eat. But it does.

And then it wants to pee, so I get out and squat half a dozen times to mark the place as mine. Larry's and mine.

Then I climb into the backseat where I've spent, I swear to god, half my life.

Just before dawn I wake up. For a second, maybe less, I'm happy again. Then I remember what happened and where I am.

I stagger out of the Volvo and follow my thirsty body up the old switchbacks on the east side of the pasture toward Mr. Tieman's place.

I find water that belongs to Boots, the yard dog. I scare him by dropping onto all fours, growling so deep in my throat that he whimpers and backs down. I drink, lapping water from his dented aluminum bowl.

Then I make my way out toward the street. It's almost light. Still some night sounds: scurrying, rustling, the hiss of big wings over my head. I crouch by the side of the road, lick a little blood from one wrist.

Twenty yards away a raccoon tries to cross the road but changes its mind, then looks at the lights bearing down on it.

The milk truck doesn't even swerve. Its taillights disappear. I raise my muzzle and test the air.

A second raccoon waddles out, sniffs the carcass, makes a wobbly circle, sniffs again, then slips back into the wood silently as a knife into water.

So that's how it's done.

Then I cry. So hard that I throw up most of what I've drunk. Then cry some more. Big sobs, not keening or howling, but huge gulping sobs.

There's no car in the driveway at Mary Ann's, but there is a light in her bedroom window. I stumble to the north side of the house; peek, or try to peek, through the windows but just bump my head. Was I stealthy before? Well, I'm not now.

I try the back door, which is open. I remember this kitchen from when we were little: a Felix clock with big round eyes that glance left on *tick,* right on *tock.* Dishes in the sink. As usual. One tomato on a white saucer. A bag of potato chips so big it looks like luggage.

"Mary Ann." The words come out but drop right to the floor. I try again: "Mary Ann!"

"Who's down there?"

I like the cranky way she answers. It's just what I need. I thought of running to Anne. But she would have said all the predictable stuff.

I hear footsteps from upstairs, follow them down a hall I also remember—all those pictures of Mary Ann's mother in her nurse's uniform: getting a diploma; shaking hands with somebody in a wheelchair, somebody with a crutch, somebody with a fake smile.

Mary Ann appears in the doorway. "Well," she says, "look what the cat dragged in."

She wears huge pajamas with the bottoms rolled up. Glasses I've never seen. A book under one arm. She reaches for a package of Winstons and a lighter. A second later smoke pours out of her nostrils. "You don't look too good, kiddo."

"I know."

She inspects me coolly, almost professionally. Then picks up the phone. Not even a hello, just "She's here, Mr. Hoagland. Yes. She's okay. She'll be home in a little while. No. I'll take care of her. It's not serious. Call the police, okay? And tell them she turned up. Then try and get some sleep." She frowns at me. "Your dad was frantic."

I sit in a kitchen chair, notice how solid that feels. I pick up a glass with something brown in the bottom and stare at it.

"Lie on the floor, okay?" When I don't she says, "I just need to get your feet higher than your head. Are you thirsty?"

I nod.

"Have you been vomiting?"

"Yes."

She helps me down onto the linoleum. She lifts my legs, hooks my feet in the rungs of a chair. I can see somebody's been sticking gum under the table.

"Did you pee this morning?"

"No. Last night I did, though. A little."

"Dry mouth?"

I move my tongue around, then nod.

"You're dehydrated."

I watch her go to the cabinet, take down two containers (one is an orange box of Arm & Hammer with its biceps like Larry's). She runs some water, mixes in a thing or two. From my place on the floor, she looks like an efficient giant.

Mary Ann puts a straw in the glass, crimps it briskly. "Sip this. A little at a time. I'm going to get you a blanket."

"I'm cold."

"I know. You're in shock, too. Slightly."

While she's gone I think about how to ask her. As long as I don't know, Larry could be sitting up in a private room watching a movie. Not lying somewhere with a sheet over him.

Mary Ann comes back, squats, drapes me with a

blanket like I'm furniture in some old house. Her face is right beside mine.

I whisper. "He's dead, isn't he?"

"No."

I cry for maybe thirty seconds. Mary Ann sits back on her heels and smokes. She cocks her head and frowns like she's thinking about buying a sofa.

"You're sure he's okay?" I ask. "When Elliot called me, he said Larry might not make—"

"I didn't say he was okay. I said he isn't dead. My mom told me they brought some hotshot trauma guy up from Springfield; he induced a little coma to let the brain rest, put in a shunt, drained that baby, and the last I heard, things were looking up."

Something that has been somewhere else funnels itself back into my body. I can feel me pouring into me through the top of my head.

"What happened, anyway?" The voice doesn't sound like mine, though.

Mary Ann shrugs. "We're never gonna know. Billy and Drew say they were driving around, saw Larry, he started something, Billy pushed him back, Larry fell and hit his head."

"Well, Jesus. Larry wouldn't—"

"Billy split, but Drew dialed 911 on his cell and stayed there until the EMT guys came." Her cool fingers look for my pulse. "He didn't move him. He just kept talking to him. Did all the right things."

"Is Billy in jail now?"

"The cops think it was an accident."

I pull the blanket tighter. "Billy always hated Larry."

Mary Ann nods. "You saw that fight at the party. Elliot said something like this was going to happen." She inhales, turns on the tap, drowns what's left of her cigarette, looks at it, drops it into a wastebasket with a smiling cow on it. "Did you guys ever do anything?"

I look up at her.

"You and Larry. Did you ever do anything or is he totally gay?"

"Once we almost did. A long time ago."

"Was it weird?"

"Kind of." There's a longish mirror under the calendar, and I watch her frown into it. "Why," I ask, "did you change your hair?"

"Oh, I got tired of that whole scene. It was just pretend, anyway. A person has to grow up sometime." She puts the back of one hand against my forehead. "You sound better. Do you feel better?"

"A little."

"Stay where you are. I'm going to heat you some soup." She opens a cabinet. "We've got tomato and chicken noodle."

"Tomato."

"Are you really going to eat it? Because I don't want to open it if you aren't going to eat it. You know how you are."

"I'm hungry."

She taps the can opener on the top of the can. "Okay then."

I watch her bare feet. She's had a pedicure. Her nails are aubergine. A word Larry would know.

She glances down at me. "It's not hard to shave your legs. You should do it. You've got nice legs. My ankles are fat." She pours soup into a big cup and opens the white microwave. "The thing is that once you start shaving, you have to do it for the rest of your life. It's like one of those millstones."

"Milestones."

"That's what I said."

I get up and put my arms around her. I can tell she wasn't expecting that. "Thanks, Mary Ann. I gotta go now. I gotta go to the hospital."

"Eat first. They won't let you in yet."

LARRY

Billy cuts me off in his ridiculous *Grapes of Wrath* truck. He literally runs me off the road, then pulls in front, trapping me.

Being scared always makes me want to pee, and—as I climb out of my car—I imagine that might work as well as Elliot's murderous thumb.

But that is almost my last smart-ass thought. Billy charges. I notice that he is bare-handed. But I hardly have time to get my feet under me, much less find my center. He's as mad as I've ever seen him. Mad as in angry. Mad as in insane.

When he plows into me, I smell Brut aftershave and I'm surprised, because I never imagined he wanted to be desirable. But of course he does. Everybody does.

Then everything seems to happen in slow motion: Drew joins the fray, pulling at Billy rather than helping him, making me grateful and surprised as I fall backward and hit the curb. Or my head does. Then I go somewhere else.

I don't hear the creak of ghostly oars, but I'm standing up in a boat. In the prow I'm afraid, like the Father of Our Country crossing the Delaware. I consciously put both hands in my pockets rather than assume George's theatrical posture.

I wonder if I'm dead. The water is smooth, covered with a few inches of flat low-lying fog like an enormous, amazingly bad meringue. I know this river (if that's what it is) isn't the Styx because there's no grim boatman. It isn't woeful Acheron or wailing Cocytus, and it certainly isn't Lethe, because Lethe is the river of forgetfulness and I remember the names of the other rivers of Hades.

The prow nudges the shore. I step off. There's less fog but more teenagers. A few are naked, some half-dressed; no one seems to know or care. A girl in a blood-drenched formal staggers past me, then a boy in torn leathers with part of his brain exposed. There's a predictable addict with one arm tied off, someone with a noose around his neck, another clutching an empty bottle of pills, a girl in a spandex aerobics outfit still wearing one of those just-two-more-I-know-you-can-do-it-you're-beautiful-inside-and-out smiles and who also has a pulpy abdominal aneurysm.

I'm not afraid. I'm not horrified or appalled. I just seem to have heartburn. Then it gets hotter, and when

I look down (I'm still wearing a shirt Kyle picked out for me), my heart is on fire.

I'm at a crossroads. A rickety sign with two rude wooden arrows points to Wendleville or First Aid. I choose, enter a triage area, kneel beside the first wounded boy, take his clammy hand, and put it into the bonfire of my heart. I watch him melt, collect in a pool at my feet, then evaporate.

Others line up behind me, but not all. Some turn their heads away. I feel they are struggling, but with what I don't know. Then I remember overhearing my mother advise a tearful client: "Don't cling to the dying," she said. "Ease their transition; don't get in the way with your own needs and regrets."

So I offer my heart to those who want it. The others, I think, return (Are returned? Choose to return?) to the world with its rolls and butter; its green beans au gratin; its beauty, mystery, and grace.

Eventually I go back to the crossroads, take a single step on the path to Wendleville, and am there. At my house. My father sits on the mud porch with the big boulder of his head in his hands. Inside, Mother washes windows frantically, which is what her mother did when my grandfather had a heart attack.

Teresa is next. (Talk about rapid transit!) I find her crying and kissing Elliot. Seriously kissing Elliot.

Like a shy maiden, I avert my eyes. I've always been sexually decorous. Being dead isn't going to change that.

I visit an anxious Stephanie, then a busy Anne. I watch Bill dress down a lazy employee and Chris cut a loaf of hot bread. Milt sits in front of Tiny Town. Luke shows a round steak to a flirty young housewife with a baby slung between her breasts.

I assume this is my farewell tour and that it's not, apparently, destined to last as long as Cher's. I've seen my parents, my two best friends, all the supernumer-aries, really. I hope I'll drop by Kyle's. Then I'll be ready.

There, in fact, is the light coming toward me—the famous light. Then I hear a voice. Not sonorous, though, or awesome. Just efficient and businesslike. "Dr. Cooperman," it says, "pick up a white courtesy phone."

The light gets closer faster, *much* closer. Then it swallows me whole like the whale swallowed reluctant Jonah.

8

...and you, and he,
and she, and so on...

ELLIOT

I can't get in to see Larry because he's got some kind of reduced coma or something like that. But I sure think about him. Just a couple of days ago, we were talking about how I felt different lately. Not like myself. And he said, "Well, let's hope whoever you are now wears the same size pants. Otherwise we'll have to go shopping." Then we laughed and I felt better.

But just thinking about somebody isn't enough. So I go over to Mary Ann's and ask her to pray with me. I'm there till, like, midnight. And just before I go home, I promise God if Larry gets well I'll stop fooling around and just use my good looks for His glory.

Next morning she calls and says there's some good news: Teresa turned up, she's on her way home, and I should make her something to eat and hightail it over there.

So I do. Turns out she doesn't want the sandwich. We end up making out a little, which I've always kind of wanted to do. But I never want to do it again (which is good), and there's no way anybody can find out (which is *very* good).

TERESA

When I get home from Mary Ann's, my father is sitting at the table stirring watery oatmeal.

"I was worried about you," he says.

"Me, too. I was worried about me, too." I've lost a shoe somewhere, one sock is worn through, and my big toe is bleeding.

"Well, you're back now."

And that's that. He goes downstairs; I make myself some soft-boiled eggs, then take a shower.

I'm standing in front of my closet wearing an old bathrobe of Mom's, a striped robe like Joseph's coat of many colors in the Bible. It's faded, but still in good shape because I never put it in the dryer. (Larry told me once, "You know that lint in the trap? That *is* your clothes.")

I'm wondering what to wear to the hospital. Larry's

mom says purple is a healing color. I have a purple tank top, so maybe that?

Just then somebody knocks like the Taliban is up the street, slams through the kitchen door, takes the stairs two at a time. I wrap the robe around me tighter, like one of those professional virgins in the Rock Hudson movies Larry liked so much. *Likes* so much. Present tense.

But it's Elliot. "I swear to god, Teresa, if something happened to you, too, I was going to kill myself."

"I'm okay, Elliot. I went to Mary Ann's and—"

"I know. She just called." He hands me something in waxed paper. "I brought you this. Where should I put it?"

"What is it?"

"Meat loaf."

"Anywhere, I guess."

He fumbles with the sandwich, puts it on the table by the bed, then takes one of my hands. And tugs. He sits down and pulls me beside him.

"I didn't sleep last night. Larry was in the hospital and you were missing."

I put my arms around him. He feels hot. He's been running. Running to me. He says, "I was so scared." Then he's kissing me, and I'm kissing him back.

I'm completely into finally making out with Elliot. But I'm thinking about that sandwich (juicy slab of meat between slices of bread white as an angel's socks), and I want it, too. I'm hungry for everything. Ravenous.

Elliot pushes me back on the bed and lies on me. This is nothing like him in the Volvo with Mary Ann or some other hootchie where it seemed like he had a kind of checklist (kiss, nibble, caress, whisper) and was cool as sherbet. No way. He's completely out of control. We start out with him on top of me, but pretty soon I'm on top of him.

I can't believe it. I'm with him at last: bony, flat-chested me.

While Elliot kisses me and keeps kissing me and fumbling with my robe, I think of a word he doesn't know—*besotted*. I feel besotted with him, and I finally understand what everybody sees in this. It's like running. Only better! And then I think, *If Larry dies, I'll settle for this.*

Suddenly he's gone. On his feet, adjusting his clothes. "Oh man," he says. "I'm sorry, Teresa."

I raise up on my elbows like someone at a swimming pool, blinking and stunned. "Are you kidding?"

He shakes his head. "No, I shouldn't have done that."

"Why not?"

"It's just wrong."

I pull my robe around me. I try to sit up, feel for the sash. He kind of collapses, partly on the floor, partly on me. We must look a little like one of those stupid old paintings: *Regret at the Feet of Virtue.*

The photographer in me tracks golden morning light through a window, my hand in his beautiful, roughed-up hair, my new smooth legs.

He pulls himself together and struggles to his feet. "I'm really sorry."

"Stop saying that."

He starts talking a mile a minute. "I'm pretty sure we can see Larry tomorrow or the day after. At least that's what Mary Ann says."

"Oh, for Christ's sake."

"I'll let you get dressed, Teresa. Then eat something. Mary Ann says you should eat. Can you eat?"

"Well, I don't know. Maybe I should ask Mary Ann."

"Don't be that way about her."

"Oh, Elliot. She stands for everything we said we didn't want."

He shakes his head. "You're not as smart as you think you are."

I grab my camera and take a picture. He's such a dead end but so gorgeous, his lips still a little bruised-looking.

LARRY

That light isn't some big New Age chariot comin' for to carry me home but an intern's penlight moving from one eye to the other, closing in, pulling back. I blink and turn away.

"Take it easy," he says. "We just got that shunt out."

"I'd like to be a little more original, but where exactly am I?"

"Wendleville Memorial Hospital. You had a close call."

"I got knocked down."

"Let me call Dr. Voss. And while I do that, your dad can come in."

I'm not unhappy in Wendleville Memorial (serving Calhoun and the surrounding counties), but I like it where I've been, too. I close my eyes, wondering if I can slip back there where my heart was on fire.

"I thought he was awake."

It's Kyle's voice. He's with, of all people, my father—Dr. Cooperman. Who puts one hand on my arm as Kyle takes my hand. I'm embarrassed. With that plus these bandages and bruises, I'm black and white and red all over, like the embarrassed zebra in that child's riddle.

"You had a close call," my father says. "They had to induce a coma."

I imagine I called him Dad when I was little, but I can't do it now.

"That sounds like fun." I don't recognize my own voice, which is muddled and thick.

"This one wouldn't go home." He puts his hand on Kyle's shoulder. "Slept out in the waiting room."

I look up at Kyle, whom no one has seen before. The Mystery Man. "What about work?" I manage. "Did you call in sick?"

"I called in alarmed."

That makes me laugh, and what a wonderful feeling it is. I like the other side, but there isn't much laughing over there. A tough crowd, as the stand-up comics say.

My father remarks, "Dr. Voss tells me you were lucky. If that other boy had decided not to hang around, we could've been looking at some serious brain injury."

"You mean Drew?" I whisper. "Drew hung around?"

"He even came by," Kyle tells me, "but they wouldn't let anybody in but your mom."

"Oh god. How's she?"

"You know your mother. Meditating. Surrounding you with that white light of hers." My father shrugs. "It can't hurt."

I sigh, one of those sighs that just escape. Then I start to cry (and I'm not sure why—for her, for him, for me, for all of us, for everybody everywhere). Kyle bends and puts his bearded cheek to mine.

My father bolts. "I'll just wait outside."

"Should I not have done that?" Kyle asks.

"He'll be all right once he shoots something small and helpless."

"That's right. He's the hunter. You know, you don't look a thing like him."

"And you don't look like yourself. You should go home and get some sleep."

"Why don't I just get in bed with you."

"Can a person talk that way in a hospital? Isn't it against the rules?"

Grinning, Kyle steps back. He always carries a rucksack, leather and very distressed. He picks that up from the chair where he must have tossed it. "We didn't," he says, "see a lot of each other before, but now I think we should."

"See more—"

"Of each other. A lot."

When I wake up, Dr. Voss is beside the bed, his brown eyes on the gadgets I'm hooked up to—or at least to the readouts from those gadgets.

"Lucky Larry," he says.

"You make me sound like one of those racing greyhounds."

"There are a couple of people to see you. Don't wear yourself out."

"I'm lying down."

"You know what I mean. Does your head hurt?"

I raise one hand and probe. Gingerly. "Just where that thing was."

"Good. If it didn't, I'd be worried."

When he opens the door, Teresa and Elliot file in.

"When you get out of here," Elliot blurts, "nothing's changed. We're still leaving the day after graduation. I'm already packing my stuff. We'll take turns driving, stay up all night. There's nothing to see till the Rockies, anyway."

What a sweet boy he is, saying things he thinks I want to hear.

Teresa strokes my arm. "What did the doctor say?"

"A few more days. Another test or two. Something ending in -*gram*."

"Not *candygram*, I imagine."

"Guess who can't stop eating?" says Elliot.

I look at Teresa, who is perched on the bed. She takes my hand, runs it up and down her impeccable calf. "And," she says, "shaving her legs."

I feel the slightest flicker of desire, like heat lightning a long way off, precursor to a storm that will never materialize. I think, *Patella, fibula, tibia*—words we learned in grade school together.

A stern nurse steps in, says that I can have only one visitor at a time. She holds the door open for Elliot, who leaves sheepishly.

I tell Teresa, "You look different."

She steps closer, kisses me, murmurs, "I'm not sur prised. I stayed up all night, drank out of a dog's bowl, shaved my legs, and then I made out with Elliot."

"Do you think if I drank out of a dog's bowl and shaved my legs he'd make out with me?"

"Don't bother. He'll just be sorry, then bore the pants off you talking about Mary Ann."

I take both her hands, pull them to my chest. "I had the most amazing dreams. My heart was on fire, and I visited a place with little lights in bassinets. If my peers get wind of this, marijuana sales will plummet and they'll all be lined up out here every weekend for one of Dr. Voss's special induced comas."

She picks up my hand and kisses every knuckle. "I'm so glad you're going to be all right."

"This guide named Mr. Bubbles told me I should work in something called the Soul Hospice."

"You almost died, sweetheart. You could have worked there permanently if it wasn't for Drew."

"*Weren't.* If it *weren't* for Drew."

"He pretty much saved your life."

"Drew did. Yes, I know. Dad told me. We should do

something for him when I get out of here. Buy him some Taco Bell gift certificates maybe."

"I can do better than that. I can get his enormous ass through the English Exit Test so he can graduate."

"We'll talk about it. In the meantime, can I caress your leg some more?"

"Why? Did getting hit in the head make you un-gay?"

Just then Elliot comes back; he holds the door for Teresa, who says, "When you're done I'll be in the cafeteria."

Elliot looks at me. Comes up to the bed. "All she does now is eat. What's up with that?"

"Eating feels good. It's life affirming. Like making out."

He looks at the floor. "I stopped before anything happened. But I shouldn't have done it at all. I promised God I'd be different if you got well."

Say, this is almost as interesting as the afterlife. "What exactly did you promise?"

"That I'd be a better person and not fool around so much. I need to settle down."

I play dumb. "With Mary Ann?"

"She's nice. Kind of fat ankles, but at least when I'm with her I know what we're talking about. With you and Teresa I'm always about ten steps behind. Do you like her?"

"Yes."

"You're not just saying that."

"Not at all."

His face lights up like I've offered him the prize from a Cracker Jack box. It moves me that my opinion matters. I could cry if I let myself. What a picture—a big fairy with a hole in his head going *boo-hoo.* What drugs did they give me, anyway—lachrymal?

"Lookit," he says, giving me a brisk heterosexual pat, "you get some rest, okay? I'll see you tomorrow. *We* will. Teresa, probably, but Mary Ann and I for sure."

He's sweet, but I'm tired of his little mystery plays: good versus evil, sybarite and puritan, penumbra and halo.

What would it be like to live somewhere on my own, I wonder. Find some kind of job, go to the movies every day, read a lot, and not get a little dog.

I'd better think about this when the drugs wear off and I'm more clearheaded, because the minute Elliot leaves, I'm asleep.

9

*...later, country and summer
buried behind us...*

ELLIOT

I'm sitting with Mary Ann, parked outside her house but not *parked* like in making out, just *parked* like in sitting still. Like in having a conversation. That kind of parked.

She's pretty in the moonlight, but, shoot, they're all pretty in the moonlight. The thing I like is, she's listening to me in the moonlight. There's nothing carnal going on. (Teresa says *carne* means meat. Real romantic, huh?)

Anyway, Mary Ann's not into that carnal stuff anymore, either. She's actually paying attention when I say, "I don't want to go to college."

"Okay. So what's the problem?"

But she doesn't say that like a smarty-pants, you know? She's not putting me down. It's not like, Poor baby doesn't want to go to the big, scary university.

She just sounds curious in a nice way. A kind of So-
tell-me-about-it way but *not* Tell-Mama-where-it-
hurts. There's a difference.

So I say, "My dad is the problem. He wants to see
me play ball for U of I."

"And you don't want to."

"I *do* want to. Who wouldn't? But I want to for
more than one semester."

She digs in her purse, offers me some gum. Which
is cool. We'll be refreshed while we hash this out. She
folds up the wrappers neatly, puts them in the ashtray.
Then asks, "Why one semester?"

"I'd flunk out, that's why."

"Ah."

That's cool, too. Not, Oh, no you wouldn't. Not if
you worked hard. Not, Of course not. You're certainly
intelligent enough—because let's face it, I am certainly
not intelligent enough, no matter how hard I work.
I followed Teresa and Elliot through high school like
some guy in a minefield walking right behind some
other guy with a map. And some teachers handed me
a good grade because I won another big game.

"I'd just ride the pine for a semester, anyway."

"Because you'd only be a freshman."

"Right. It's not like I'd make the varsity."

"And your dad won't listen to reason?"

"Are you . . . kidding?" I almost swore, but Mom's
right—it's disrespectful. "He'd go ballistic."

She shrugs. I like to see girls shrug. Why is that?

"What goes up," Mary Ann says, "must come down."

"Meaning Dad?"

She just nods. "And your mom doesn't want you to go, anyway."

"How do you know that?"

"I ran into her in Kroger's last week and we had a little chat."

Now, that's something I'd like to see: Mary Ann and Mom chatting at the grocery store. Not necessarily about me, either. Just chatting. Passing the time together.

"So," Mary Ann says, "you've got an ally in your mother."

"She said that?"

"She just wants what's best for you." Mary Ann leans forward. "What do you really want to do?"

I honest-to-god sigh. "Not waste a semester pretending something that isn't going to happen is."

She squirms a little, tucks one leg under. Her ankles aren't that fat.

"That's what you *don't* want. I asked what you want."

"I'm a pretty good butcher. I'm good with customers and I like cutting meat, because when you leave the shop, that's that. It's not like some pork chop is going to call you at home."

Mary Ann laughs, which I really like. I'm never funny with Teresa or Larry. They're the witty ones.

"Could you," she asks, "work for your dad? Or would you have to get a job somewhere else?"

"No way could I go somewhere else. Sure, he'd put me to work; he'd just be . . ." I look for the word, which to me is usually like turning over pieces of those jig-saw puzzles that are all sky.

"Difficult?"

"Yeah, exactly."

"He'd have more time off with you there."

"That's true."

"He could come in when he wanted, knock off early. Who wouldn't want that?"

"It sounds easy when you say it."

"Just sit down with them, Elliot. Like at the kitchen table. Look them in the eye. State your case."

I love that. *State my case.*

Mary Ann glances at her house. "I gotta go. Tests day after tomorrow." She pretends to look exasperated, but I can tell she likes it, too. Likes taking tests because she probably aces them now.

"Are your classes hard?" I ask.

"Chemistry is." That cute shrug again. "But it'll be worth it."

She reaches for the handle. I hop out, zoom around the car, open the door. She puts one hand up.

"We're taking this slow, remember?"

I remember, but I don't step back. She smells good. And not, like Larry said about some girl, "competi-tively fragrant." Just clean.

TERESA

When Drew comes over to study for the English Exit
Test, he's wearing Goliath's jeans and Pinocchio's hat.
But he smells like coconut and chocolate. While I'm
opening a book or looking for a pencil, he unwraps an
Almond Joy from some deep stash of Almond Joys and
feeds it into his mouth like somebody stoking a boiler.

"Want to start?" I ask.

He shrugs. "Can we have the radio on? I like to
study with the radio on."

I get up, turn the black dial on the red radio and
get the Rolling Stones, still wanting to spend the night
with somebody but—at their age—probably just to get
some sleep.

I tell him, "My mother loved those guys."

"Mine, too. Then she split and Dad got married
again. Now I gotta listen to elevator music."

"I didn't know your mom ran away."

"Yeah."

"Where'd she go?"

He shrugs. "Who knows?"

I try to remember if I ever heard him talk this much before today: Billy had a mouth big enough for both of them. But Drew must have said something sometime; we were in a couple of classes together. I just wasn't listening. I mean, who was he? Not Elliot or Larry.

"Where do you want to start?"

"Wherever. I'm pretty far behind."

"Why? Did you not understand?"

"Can I have something to eat?"

"After we finish."

He takes a big breath and lets it out again. "You want the truth about why? It's because Billy said it wasn't cool to get good grades. I had to show him my report card."

"So he was like some sort of anti-dad: The worse you did, the more he liked it?"

Drew nods.

"Why did you go along with that?"

"It was better than being by myself. C'mon. What would you have done with Larry and Elliot?"

I'm about to say it was different. But I don't. It wasn't that different.

I take out a photocopied sheet. "Let's try simile and metaphor."

"Okay. I kind of remember those. Billy couldn't stop me from listening in class."

"What's his story?"

"Billy's? I don't know anymore. He's still around, mouthing off."

I push the sheet toward Drew. "Just fill in the blanks and then we'll talk about them."

"Read 'em to me, okay? I got something in my eye riding over here."

It's not true, but I let it pass. "Okay, here goes—'In his rage, my father would pound on the wall like . . .'" I look up expectantly.

"Milton's a craftsman, isn't he?"

At first I think he means John Milton of *Paradise Lost*. Then, "Oh, you're talking about my dad. How'd you know about him?"

"From the Hobby Shop. I bought this remote control car to race and crash and stuff. I heard some guys talking."

"Let's forget about my dad and just get you through the exit test."

"Okay. Well, you know: '. . . pound on the wall *like a drum*' is what everybody's going to say, and *'like a madman'* is just so-so. *'Like a gorilla'* is pretty good, I think, and in my case it's right on the money, because my dad's got so much hair on his back he looks like he's wearing a sweater." He squints so hard it makes my face hurt.

"You need glasses, don't you?"

"I guess. I get along. Do the next one."

"'In her wedding gown, the bride looked like . . .'"

"Are you gonna get married, Teresa?"

"Not until we finish this exercise, and the way it's going . . ."

"Very funny."

"I don't know, Drew."

"You can't marry Elliot, can you? He's got Mary Ann."

"Can we just do the simile, please."

"And Larry's got that homo in Springfield."

"Will you just forget about who's not marrying whom?"

"Okay."

"I mean it."

"I said okay."

I shuffle some papers like some ditzy anchorwoman on TV. "Let's do the melting pot."

"I thought you said we couldn't eat till after."

"Ha-ha. Do you know what a melting pot is?"

"A big pot stuff melts in?"

"Well, they're going to ask you to write about whether America is a melting pot or not."

"So should I do it now?"

I look at the notebook he brought. It's gray and as wrinkled as the log of the *Titanic*. "Just tell me."

He takes off that hat. He and Billy shaved their heads, but Drew's blond hair is starting to grow back already.

"Well, the answer is no. I mean the blacks stick together and so do the Italians. And the dopers and the
Goths. Everybody mixes but nobody melts."

"That's good. Write something like that and you'll
be okay."

He sits up straighter. "I've been talking to that
counselor at school, Ms. Williams, and she said I've got
potential. She said Billy was a bad influence on me.
You know what that's like. Larry and Elliot held you
back, too."

I glare at him. "What's that supposed to mean—
held me back?"

"Are you kidding? I mean who do you know besides them? You guys had this kind of private club nobody else could get into."

"Except for Elliot's girlfriends." I hear the edge in
my voice.

Drew shakes his head. "They just had guest passes."
He runs one hand up under his T-shirt and scratches.
"You really screwed up. You're smart and you're pretty
nice. You could have had a thousand friends."

I stand up, grab the radio, and twist the dial. Some
deejay croons the names of the next couple of songs:
"Some Enchanted Evening" and "Be Careful, It's My
Heart." I should find the punk station: "Another
Fucked-Up Night" and "Watch Out! That's My Boner."

I head for the refrigerator, take out everything I
need for a sandwich. A *huge* sandwich: Roman Meal

bread, bologna, salami, two kinds of cheese, lettuce, sliced tomato. Half to him, half to me. And two glasses of milk.

Who cares who I'm not going to marry? Who cares who was a bad influence or how many friends I could have had? I just want to eat. Drew breathes harder. His eyes half close. I should take a picture. Call it *Rapture of the Teeth*. But look who's talking. I wish I'd made two sandwiches. Or a bigger one.

We're just about finished when my dad starts up from the underworld. His footsteps are, I have to admit, a little ominous. Drew stops chewing. Wipes his mouth with a paper napkin.

"That's not Elliot, is it? He's not going to kick my ass, is he? I was the one who stayed with—"

"Well, hello. I'm Milt Hoagland, Teresa's father." He offers to shake hands. I think, *Would you buy a used car from this man?*

Drew stands up and clutches his hat at waist level— a move right out of one of those I've-come-to-you-my-lord-because-the-other-serfs-are-stealing-my-sheep movies. Drew shakes hands shyly, introduces himself, and stutters, "I know who you are. F-f-from the Hobby Shop. You're, like, a legend."

My dad looks at his craftsman's hands. "Oh, I wouldn't say that."

"No, really."

My father notices me. "Are you two taking a break, sweetheart? There are Cokes in the refrigerator."

Sweetheart? "We're studying, Dad."

"When you're finished, then," he says, "there's something downstairs Drew might be interested in."

Drew gasps. "Tiny Town? Man, I would love to see Tiny Town."

"What about graduating?" I ask.

Drew looks from me to my dad and back again.

"It'd just take a minute, Teresa." My dad puts one hand on the back of Drew's chair like they're posing for a photographer at the Good Citizenship awards.

They clomp down the stairs together, leaving me alone like the comic strip orphan I'm named after, one Terry of *Terry and the Pirates.*

Fine. If I was even a little worried about abandoning my father, that's gone.

Still, when I hear them talking down there, I want to slap them so hard their ears bleed. Then the trains start: a little chug, a little melancholy wail. Drew's boogery laugh is followed by what I'll bet is his favorite compliment: "This is so cool."

My back to the wall, I sink to the floor. I can't call Larry; he's in Springfield with Kyle. Elliot's six blocks away with Mary Ann.

My camera is on the counter, so I get to my feet, grab it, turn it on myself, check the little preview screen. I look awful, but the picture's good. That's what matters.

LARRY

Deep summer wears its big green necklace. Boys like Elliot and I used to be prowl the creeks looking for arrowheads.

I spend a lot of time with Kyle and his friends. Teresa's halfway through some reading list from Boston College. Since Elliot's helping his dad then picking up his mom and Mary Ann so the four of them can all have dinner together at the Outback, can the bridal registry at Target be far behind?

But today just the three of us are eating barbecue at a picnic table—splintered, stained, dangerous—at a stand about twenty miles from Wendleville. Ribs are somebody's afterthought, really, because the draws here are tomatoes and corn, zucchini and beets, fresh eggs and watermelon.

The place is called, I'm afraid, Old MacDonald's Farm. Teresa warned Elliot not to say *E-I-E-I-O* under any circumstances. But the people who drive all the way from Springfield in their aw-shucks togs from L.L. Bean can't resist. Everywhere a *cluck-cluck*.

Teresa has powered through her slab of short ribs and is staring at Elliot's. "You aren't going to let those go to waste, are you?"

"How can you guys eat at a time like this?"

I remind him, "It's not the Last Supper, my friend."

"It sort of is. We're never going to see each other again."

Teresa points out, "We only graduated a month ago. There's almost the whole summer."

"Two lousy months. Not even. Teresa leaves for school in August, and you start in a week."

I shrug. "Community colleges run all year round."

He looks at Teresa but asks about me. "What's he want to be again?"

Teresa wipes sauce from her impudent lips with a napkin. "He wants to be a PA. And in this case," she adds, "that doesn't stand for *public address* system, either. It's *physician's assistant.*"

"Why does he want to be that?"

Teresa points at me. "Well, look. Here he is now. Let's ask him."

"I don't know, Elliot. I had this dream in the hospital. I can always change my mind." I put one hand on his forearm. He covers mine with his.

"You're going to move to Springfield, aren't you, Larry?"

"No. I don't know."

"See!" He takes his hand away.

"I probably won't. I only have classes two nights a week. Mary Ann has the same schedule and she didn't move to Springfield."

"Yeah? Well, Mary Ann doesn't have a boyfriend with an apartment." He frowns. "What does Kyle do again?"

"He works for the gas company."

"And he's gay."

"Yes."

"A gay gas man."

"I admit it sounds worse when you say it."

Teresa reaches across the table and pulls Elliot's paper plate toward her.

"Just tell me this before you move away forever, okay?" he demands. "Who else that we know is queer?"

Teresa, who's cutting a tomato in half with my pocketknife, laughs out loud.

"What?" he demands.

"I'm going to miss you, Elliot." She kisses him— a big, smeary barbecue kiss. Then she advises me, "Humor him."

So I say, "In our class I'm the only one. But there are a couple of guys in eleventh grade. And one girl."

"Oh god. Don't tell me. Who's the girl?"

Teresa asks, not unreasonably, "What do you care?"

"I could have," he says, "saved her."

Teresa stands up. "I thought about being a lesbian," she says, "but decided against it." She heads for a horse trough full of ice and watermelon. Then stops, turns, and delivers the punch line. "Too many forms to fill out."

"She's kidding, right?"

I nod.

He moves closer. The air has a now-that-we're-alone quality. Sure enough: "I'm not sure I can do it, man."

"What are we talking about, Elliot?"

"Mary Ann. I'm not sure I can, you know, just be with her. There's these twins at church. And this friend of Mary Ann's from the community college who's just killer."

"I know what you mean. Kyle's nice, but the more I see of him, the less there is to see."

"There you go! Absolutely. So don't move to Springfield. I mean it. Stay here and we'll play the field."

When Teresa returns with half a watermelon, she sits between us this time: boy girl boy.

Elliot booms, "So who are those two queer guys?"

He's loud so that she will know we've been talking about something else, something she isn't part of. She just puts the watermelon down and cuts it deftly. "I like this knife. I'm going to get me a knife."

"C'mon, Larry. Who are they?"

Teresa doesn't look at me. "At least tell him about the exceptional salad."

"'Exceptional salad'? What's an exceptional salad got to do with anything?" Elliot has a prissy way of picking at one barbecued rib with two fingers.

"Kyle and I had dinner with some friends of his, these guys in their fifties, okay?"

"Oh my god . . ."

Teresa and I stare at him.

"You mean," Elliot says, "that you don't outgrow it and you're gay forever?"

Teresa's eyes narrow. "You've got to be kidding, Elliot."

He's so smug. "I had you going for a minute, didn't I? Mary Ann says I've got a great sense of humor."

"And she would know," Teresa mutters, "with her upcoming special on Comedy Central."

But he's immune to her for the moment. "Tell me about that salad."

"These guys were just saying that thirty or forty years ago, there was all this code for somebody who was gay. 'He's difficult' was one. 'The family's having problems with him' was another one. But my favorite—"

"*Our* favorite," Teresa insists.

"—was 'He makes an exceptional salad.'"

"So what is it now?"

I shrug. "Pretty much like the T-shirt says: *I'm Queer—Deal with It.*"

Elliot scowls. "Drew's not, is he?"

Teresa buries her face in a wedge of watermelon, then surfaces, wipes away the juice with yet another napkin, and answers for me. "No."

"Are you sure? First there was Billy, and now he's hooked up with your dad. Doesn't that tell you something?"

"He's fat and lonely, okay, Elliot? They go to the model shop together. Jesus."

I pick up her hand, the relatively clean one. I raise it to my lips gallantly.

"Don't," she says, "make me cry, you big fairy."

An hour or so later, we drop Elliot off first. He cuffs me around; Teresa he kisses on the (I notice, not unwilling) lips. "I'll call you guys tomorrow. We'll do something."

He stands on his lawn and watches until we turn a corner. Teresa rubs the back of my neck, toys with my hair. Nobody's talking. There are clouds in the west and distant thunder that sounds like someone moving heavy furniture.

Drew's bicycle is outside her house, not locked, just leaning against the porch. She slides across the seat, kisses me good-bye. Holds on longer than usual.

I wait until she's inside, then ease away. I'm not anxious to go home, so I take the longer way, that street where Billy ambushed me, the one that runs by the now wide road leading to Lakeview Acres.

It's dusk, the best time of day to see the homes there. Two of the finished ones have lights on, which makes them seem to float like houseboats.

There's Kyle, there's college, and there's lunch with my dad at the club every Wednesday. But part of me still wants California. I could backtrack, pick up my friends. I wouldn't have to talk them into anything, not really. I'll bet they'd go in a heartbeat.